This book belongs to

....

Illustrated Treasury of
Christmas
Stories

Compiled by Tig Thomas

Miles
Kelly

First published in 2014 by Miles Kelly Publishing Ltd
Harding's Barn, Bardfield End Green, Thaxted, Essex, CM6 3PX, UK

This edition published 2016

2 4 6 8 10 9 7 5 3 1

Publishing Director Belinda Gallagher
Creative Director Jo Cowan
Editorial Director Rosie Neave
Senior Editor Sarah Parkin
Designer Joe Jones
Cover Designer Jo Cowan
Production Elizabeth Collins, Caroline Kelly
Reprographics Stephan Davis, Jennifer Cozens, Thom Allaway
Assets Lorraine King

ISBN 978-1-78209-988-8

Printed in China

British Library Cataloguing-in-Publication Data
A catalogue record for this book is available from the British Library

ACKNOWLEDGEMENTS
The publishers would like to thank the following artists
who have contributed to this book:

Cover: Claudia Venturini (Plum Pudding Illustration Agency)
Inside pages: Tamsin Hinrichsen, Natalia Moore (Advocate Art);
Charlotte Cooke (The Bright Agency); Rachel Cloyne (Pickled Ink);
Florencia Denis, Simona Sanfilippo, Antonia Woodward
(Plum Pudding Illustration Agency)

Made with paper from a sustainable forest

www.mileskelly.net

CONTENTS

CHRISTMAS IS COMING

MAGICAL MOMENTS

WINTER WONDERLAND

PRESENTS AND PARTIES

GOODWILL AND GIVING

ABOUT THE AUTHORS

Find information below on some of the authors whose stories appear in this book.

Louisa May Alcott
1832-1888

Little Women is Louisa May Alcott's most famous book. She began it in the hope it might pay off some of her family's debts. In it, she told stories from her own childhood with her sisters May, Elizabeth and Anna. It was an enormous success and she became both wealthy and an unwilling celebrity.

Hans Christian Andersen
1805-1875

Born in Denmark, Hans Christian Andersen was apprenticed to a weaver and a tailor, before working as an actor and singer in Copenhagen. While in the theatre he wrote poetry and stories, and became famous worldwide for children's tales. These have been translated into over 150 languages, and have inspired movies, plays and ballets.

L. Frank Baum
1856-1919

Lyman Frank Baum was born in New York, USA. He hated his first name and preferred to be called Frank. Baum's greatest success was *The Wonderful Wizard of Oz*. He went on to write 13 books about the magical land of Oz, and many other short stories, poems and scripts.

Charles Dickens
1812-1870

When Dickens was ten years old his father was imprisoned for debt, and the young boy was put to work in a factory, pasting labels on glue bottles. This early experience helped to make him a passionate social reformer, using his hugely popular novels to expose the terrible conditions for poor people at the time.

About the Authors

Kenneth Grahame
1859-1932

Grahame was born in Edinburgh, Scotland. His mother died when he was five, and he and his siblings were raised by their grandmother. Unable to afford to go to university, Grahame took a job in the Bank of England. He began to write about the characters that would later appear in *The Wind in the Willows*, one of the most beloved children's books, in letters to his son.

Johnny Gruelle
1880-1938

Artist and author Johnny Gruelle started to write and paint his famous Raggedy Ann books after his daughter, Marcella, found a dusty, faceless doll in the attic. He painted a face on the doll and Marcella played with it so much that he thought other children might like to read about it.

L M Montgomery
1874-1942

Lucy Maude Montgomery's mother died
when she was two and she was sent to live
with her grandparents on Prince Edward Island,
Canada. Her best-known character, Anne of
Green Gables, seems to have been based on
Montgomery herself.

Clement Clarke Moore
1779-1863

A Professor of Biblical Learning,
Clement Clarke Moore was rather
embarrassed when he became best known for
writing the poem often called 'The Night before
Christmas', although its proper name is 'A Visit
from Saint Nicholas'. It has been described as
the most famous piece of poetry ever
written by an American.

ABOUT THE ARTISTS

Rachel Cloyne can't remember not drawing. Her degree in Illustration at Brighton University and books that she self-published have led her to working on book jackets, and picture and pop-up books. Rachel combines ink and computer techniques to create intricate, detailed images.

Decorative frames

Charlotte Cooke has loved drawing since she was a little girl. She enjoys making up adventures and seeing them come alive in her pictures. Charlotte lives near the sea with her husband and two children, and eats ice cream on the beach as often as possible.

Cutting the Christmas Tree • Jimmy Scarecrow's Christmas • Jimmieboy's Snowman
The Christmas Party • The Josephs' Christmas • Little Women's Christmas Breakfast

Florencia Denis began illustrating children's books when she started to read tales to her own children. She has been published in Argentina and the United Kingdom. Florencia just needs watercolours, pencils, ink and music to work.

Matthew Insists on Puffed Sleeves • Christmas Every Day • Christmas Under
the Snow • Kate and Dick's Christmas • The First Stockings • The Christmas Cuckoo

Tamsin Hinrichsen illustrates children's books from her loft studio in Cape Town, South Africa. She works in acrylics on paper, and particularly likes to paint folk tales and animal stories.

Jesus is Born in Bethlehem

About the Artists

Natalia Moore is a qualified art teacher and freelance illustrator. She works with mixed media and puts in the finishing touches digitally. Natalia likes to draw from real-life and is never without her sketchbook.

The First Christmas Tree • Little Roger's Night in the Church • How Johnny Cricket Saw Santa Claus • Making Angels in the Snow • Katy and Clover's Christmas • The Cratchits' Christmas Goose • Aunt Cyrilla's Christmas Basket

Simona Sanfilippo loves working on illustrations full of emotions and colours. She decided to follow the path into the children's book world after studying illustration at IED in Turin, Italy.

The Elves and the Shoemaker • The Nutcracker and the Mouse King Raggedy Andy's Smile • The Beavers' Christmas Tree • Thank You Letters The Little Match Girl • Scrooge Celebrates Christmas

Antonia Woodward loved drawing beautiful pictures and turning them into miniature books as a little girl. She combines paint, pencil and collage to create her gentle illustrations.

A Christmas Star • Santa Claus' Helpers • A Christmas Tree Adventure The Wild Wood in Winter • Christmas Morning • Mr Dog Plays Santa Claus

13

14

CHRISTMAS IS COMING

Jesus is Born in Bethlehem

Anon

*Christmas is traditionally the time when Christians
celebrate the birth of Jesus, who they believe is the son of God.
This is the story of what happened when Jesus was born.*

A young woman called Mary lived in the town of Nazareth, among the hills of Galilee. She was going to be married to a carpenter called Joseph, who, like herself, lived in Nazareth.

One day God sent the angel Gabriel to

Mary with a message. Mary, when she saw and heard the angel, was a little frightened but the angel told her he had some good news for her. The Son of God was coming into the world very soon, and he would be born as Mary's little child. And Gabriel said that when he was born, Mary should call him Jesus.

About this time Caesar Augustus, the great Emperor of Rome, sent word to Herod, his ruler in Palestine, that he was to take a census of the Jews. Everybody's name had to be written down, as well as their age and many other things about them. Every twenty years Augustus had a census taken, so that he might know how much money the Jews ought to pay him in taxes, and how many soldiers he could demand they send him.

At census time, people had to go to their home towns where their fathers' fathers lived a long time ago, and had to register there instead of in the homes where they lived now.

Now, both Joseph and Mary belonged to the family of the great King David, who was born in Bethlehem. So Mary had to prepare for a long journey, and go with her husband to Bethlehem. She rode on a donkey and Joseph led it

carefully over the rough roads.

Bethlehem is on top of a hill, and people have to climb up a steep road to get into the town. When Joseph and Mary reached Bethlehem, Mary was very tired, and so Joseph went to look for an inn in which they could stay the night. An inn is a large house that people stay at when they are on a journey. There were many inns in Bethlehem, but Mary and Joseph, after their long journey from Nazareth, could not find one that had room.

In the end, one innkeeper said he had no rooms for them, but, if they wanted, they could sleep in the stable with the animals. And because there was no room for them in the inn, Mary and Joseph had to go into that stable to sleep, and in that stable Jesus was born. Mary wrapped him in swaddling

cloths, which were strips of cloth wound snugly round him to help him feel warm and safe, and she laid him in a manger, the place where the animals' food is put.

On the hill where Bethlehem stood, shepherds took their flocks to feed. There were wild animals in Palestine, and all night long the shepherds of Bethlehem watched to see that no harm came to their sheep.

That night an angel of the Lord appeared to them and a bright light shone round about them. The shepherds were terrified, but the angel said, "Don't be afraid, I've come to tell you wonderful news. A king has been born this night in the city of David. You will find the baby wrapped in swaddling cloths and lying in a manger."

And then the sky was filled with a wonderful light, and angels singing, "Glory to God in the highest, and on Earth peace, good will towards men."

When the light faded, the song ended and the angels returned to heaven, the shepherds climbed quickly over the hillside to Bethlehem. And there, in the stable near the inn, they found Mary and Joseph, and the baby lying in the manger, as the angels had said.

Jesus had some other visitors too. A long way on the eastern side of the River Jordan, there were countries where people used to watch the Sun and the Moon and the stars very carefully. If they saw anything new and strange in the heavens, they thought it meant that something wonderful was going to happen on Earth.

One day these wise men saw a bright star that they had never seen before. And as they looked at it they felt sure that its message was that a great King of the Jews had been born in Judaea, a person they called the Christ. So they took expensive gifts of gold and sweet-smelling stuff – such as people gave to kings in those days – and they loaded their camels, and left their homes, and rode for many weeks till they came to Jerusalem.

When they got there they said, "Where is he that is born King of the Jews? For we have seen his star in the East, and have come to worship him."

When Herod the ruler heard about these wise men he was troubled. He didn't want any kings coming along who might challenge him. He sent for the best priests, and other clever men, and asked them where Christ would be born.

They said to him, "In Bethlehem of Judaea." They had read this in the Bible.

Then Herod said to the wise men, "Go and search out the young child, and when you have found him, come back and tell me where he is, so that I may come and see him also." But really he planned to kill Jesus.

The wise men agreed and then they went away to Bethlehem. The bright star led them on till it stopped above the place where the baby Jesus was.

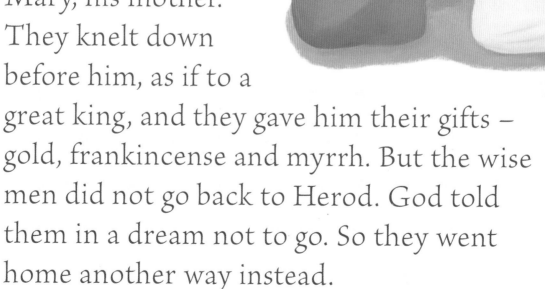

When they came into the house (there was room in the inn now) they saw the baby with Mary, his mother. They knelt down before him, as if to a great king, and they gave him their gifts – gold, frankincense and myrrh. But the wise men did not go back to Herod. God told them in a dream not to go. So they went home another way instead.

But the danger of Herod finding out about Jesus was still there. So after the wise men were gone, God's angel came to Joseph in his sleep, and said to him, "Take the baby and his mother, and escape into Egypt, for Herod will seek the child to kill him."

So Joseph at once got up, and took Jesus and Mary and put them on his donkey. He led them quietly out of Bethlehem and away to Egypt, where they would be safe.

The First Christmas Tree

An extract from *The Life and Adventures of Santa Claus*
by L Frank Baum

*This is part of a story telling how Santa Claus
lives in a place called Laughing Valley, but goes out
into the world to bring joy to children.*

*C*laus had always kept his promise,
returning to the Laughing Valley by
daybreak, but only the swiftness of his
reindeer has enabled him to do this, for he
travels all over the world.

He loved his work and he loved the brisk

night ride on his sledge and the gay tinkle of the sleigh bells. On that first trip with the ten reindeer only Glossie and Flossie wore bells, but each year after for eight years Claus carried presents to the children of the Gnome King, and that good-natured monarch gave him in return a string of bells at each visit, so that finally every one of the ten deer was supplied. You may imagine what a merry tune the bells played as the sledge sped over the snow.

The children's stockings were so long that it required a great many toys to fill them, and soon Claus found there were other things besides toys that children love.

So he sent some of the fairies, who were always his good friends, into the Tropics. They returned with great bags full of oranges and bananas that they had plucked

from the trees. And other fairies flew to the wonderful Valley of Phunnyland, where delicious candies and bonbons grew thickly

on the bushes, and returned laden with many boxes of sweetmeats for the little ones. On each Christmas Eve, Santa Claus placed these things in the long stockings, together with his toys, and the children were glad to get them, you may be sure.

There are also warm countries where there is no snow in winter, but Claus visited them as well as the colder countries, for there were little wheels inside the runners of his sledge that permitted it to run as smoothly over bare ground as on the snow. And the children who lived in the warm countries learned to know the name of Santa Claus as well as those who lived nearer to the Laughing Valley.

Once, just as the reindeer were ready to start on their yearly trip, a fairy came to Claus and told him of three little children who lived beneath a rough tent of skins on a broad plain, where there were no trees. These poor children were miserable and unhappy, for their parents neglected them. Claus decided to visit these children before

he returned home, and during his ride he picked up the bushy top of a pine tree, which the wind had broken off, and placed it in his sledge.

It was nearly morning when the reindeer stopped before the lonely tent of skins where the poor children lay asleep. Claus planted the bit of pine tree in the sand and stuck many candles on the branches. Then he hung some of his prettiest toys on the tree, as well as several bags of candies.

The First Christmas Tree

It did not take long to do all this, for Santa Claus works quickly, and when all was ready he lit the candles and, thrusting his head in at the opening of the tent, he shouted, "Merry Christmas little ones!"

With that he leapt into his sledge and was out of sight before the children, rubbing the sleep from their eyes, could come out to see who had called them.

You can imagine the wonder and joy of those little ones, who had never in their lives known a real pleasure before, when they saw the tree, sparkling with lights that shone brilliant in the grey dawn and hung with toys enough to make them happy

for years to come.

They joined hands and danced around the tree, shouting and laughing, until they were obliged to pause for breath. And their parents also came out to look and wonder, and thereafter had more respect and consideration for their children, since Santa Claus had honoured them with such beautiful gifts.

The idea of the Christmas tree pleased Claus, and so the following year he carried many of them in his sledge and set them up in the homes of poor people who seldom saw trees, and placed candles and toys on the branches.

Of course he could not carry enough trees in one load for all who wanted them, but in some homes the fathers were able to get trees and have them all ready for Santa

Claus when he arrived. And these Claus always decorated as prettily as possible, and hung with toys enough for all the children who came to see the tree lit.

These ideas and the generous manner in which they were carried out made the children long for that one night in the year when their friend Santa Claus should visit them. As such anticipation is very pleasant and comforting, the little ones gleaned much happiness by wondering what would happen when Santa Claus next arrived.

The Elves and the Shoemaker

Traditional story

*T*here was once a shoemaker who, through no fault of his own, had become so poor that at last he had only leather enough left for one pair of shoes.

It was the month before Christmas, when parties were starting to be held, and he planned a pair of dancing shoes for a young lady. In the evening he cut out the shoes, which he intended to begin upon the next morning, and then, feeling tired and worried, he lay down quietly, said his prayers and fell asleep.

In the morning, when he was preparing to sit down to work, he found the pair of shoes standing finished on his table. He was amazed, and could not understand it in the least.

He took the shoes in his hand to examine them more closely. They were so neatly sewn that not a stitch was out of place, and were as good as the work of a master-hand.

Soon after that, a young girl came in and, as she was so pleased with the shoes, she paid more than the ordinary price for them. So the shoemaker was able to buy leather for two pairs with the money.

He cut them out in the evening, and next day, with fresh courage, was about to go to work. But he had no need to, for when he got up, the shoes were finished, and two more people eagerly bought them. That gave him so much money that he was able to buy leather for four pairs of shoes.

Early next morning he found the four pairs finished, and so it went on – what he cut out in the evening was finished in the morning. In a couple of weeks the shoemaker was living very comfortably, with plenty of money for food, and even enough to buy himself and his wife fine new clothes.

Now, it happened on the day before Christmas, when he had cut out shoes, that he said to his wife, "How would it be if we were to sit up tonight to see who it is that lends us such a helping hand?"

His wife agreed, lit a candle, and then they both hid themselves in the corner of the room behind the clothes that were hanging there.

At midnight there came two little raggedy men, who sat down at the shoemaker's table, took up the cut-out work, and began with their tiny fingers to stitch, sew and hammer so neatly and quickly, that the shoemaker could not believe his eyes. They did not stop till everything was finished and stood complete on the table, then they ran swiftly away.

The next day his wife said, "The little men have made us rich, and we ought to show them how grateful we are. Let us give them a Christmas present, for tomorrow is

Christmas Day. I will make them little shirts, coats, waistcoats and trousers, and will even knit them strong socks, and you shall make them each a pair of shoes."

The shoemaker agreed, and in the evening, when they had everything ready, they laid out the presents on the table with wine and cake, and hid themselves to see how the little men would behave.

At midnight they came skipping in, and were about to set to work, but, instead of the leather ready cut out, they found the charming little clothes.

At first they were surprised, then extremely delighted. With the greatest speed they put on and smoothed down the pretty clothes, singing,

"Now we're dressed so fine and neat,
Why cobble more for others' feet?"

Then they drank the wine and ate the cake, and hopped and danced about, and leaped over chairs and tables, and then out at the door.

The next day was Christmas Day, and they did not appear, nor any day after that, but the shoemaker did well as long as he lived and had good luck in everything he did. And every Christmas Eve after that, he and his wife poured a glass of wine and drank a toast to their secret helpers.

A Christmas Star

Adapted from a story
by Katharine Pyle

"Come now, my dear little stars," said Mother Moon. "I will tell you a story." Every morning for a week before Christmas, Mother Moon used to call all the little stars around her and tell them stories about wonderful stars. Then the stars would bid Mother Moon goodnight and go to bed in the sky chamber, for the stars' bedtime is when people down on Earth are beginning to waken and see that

it is morning.

But that particular morning, one golden star still lingered beside Mother Moon.

"What is the matter, my little star?" asked Mother Moon.

"Oh, Mother Moon," said the golden star. "I am so sad! I wish I could shine for someone's heart like that star of wonder that you tell us about."

"Why, aren't you happy up here in the sky country?" asked Mother Moon.

"Yes," said the star, "but tonight it seems as if I must find some heart to shine for."

"Then if that is so," said Mother Moon, "the time has come, my little star, for you to go through the Wonder Hall."

"The Wonder Hall? What is that?" asked the star.

Rising, Mother Moon took the little star

by the hand and led it to a door that it had never seen before. Mother Moon opened the door and there was a long dark hall. At the far end shone a little speck of light.

"What is this?" asked the star.

"It is the Wonder Hall, and it is through this that you must go to find the heart where you belong," said Mother Moon.

So the little star stepped into the Wonder Hall, and the door of the sky house closed behind it.

The next thing the star knew it was hanging in a toy shop with a whole row of other stars, which were blue and red and silver. The little star itself was gold.

The shop smelled of evergreen, and was full of Christmas shoppers, men and women and children.

But of them all, the star looked at no one

but a little boy standing in front of the counter, for as soon as the star saw the child it knew that he was the one to whom it belonged.

The little boy was standing beside a sweet-faced woman and he was not looking at anything in particular. The star shook and trembled on the string that held it, because it was afraid the child would not see it.

The lady had a number of toys on the counter before her, and she was saying, "Now I think we have presents for everyone. There's the doll for Lou, and the game for Ned, and the music box for May, and then the rocking horse and the sled."

Suddenly the little boy caught her by the

44

arm. "Oh, mother," he said. He had just seen the star.

"Well, what is it darling?" asked the lady.

"Oh, mother, just see that star up there! I wish – oh, I do wish I had it."

"Oh, my dear, we have so many things for the Christmas tree," said the mother.

"Yes, I know, but I do want the star," said the child.

"Very well," said the mother, smiling, "then we will take that, too."

So the star was taken down from where it hung and wrapped up in a piece of paper, and all the while it thrilled with joy, for now it belonged to the little boy.

It was not until the afternoon before Christmas, when the tree was being decorated, that the golden star was unwrapped and taken out from the paper.

CHRISTMAS IS COMING

"Here is something else," said the sweet-faced lady. "We must hang this on the tree."

"Oh, yes," said someone else who was helping to decorate the tree, "we will hang it here on the very top."

So the little star hung on the highest branch of the Christmas tree.

That evening all the candles were lit on the Christmas tree. The gold and silver balls, the fairies and the glass fruits shone and twinkled in the light, and high above them all shone the golden star.

A Christmas Star

At seven o'clock the folding doors
of the room where the Christmas
tree stood were thrown open, and a
crowd of children came trooping in.
They laughed and shouted and all
talked together, and after a while there
was music, and then presents were
taken from the tree and given to
all of them.

The star had never been so
happy in all its life, for the little
boy was there.

The little boy stood apart
from the other children,
looking up at the star with his
hands clasped behind him.

At last it was all over.
The lights were put out, the
children went home and the house grew

still. Then the ornaments on the tree began to talk among themselves.

"So that is all over," said a silver ball.

"Yes," said a glass bunch of grapes, "the best of it is over. Of course people will come to look at us for several days yet, but it won't be like this evening."

"And then I suppose we'll be laid away for another year," said a paper fairy. "Really it seems hardly worthwhile. Such a few days out of the year and then to be shut up in the dark box again."

The bunch of grapes was wrong in saying that people would come to look at the Christmas tree the next few days, for it stood neglected and nobody came near it. Everybody in the house went about very quietly, with anxious faces, for the little boy was ill.

At last, one evening, a nurse came into the room and took the golden star. She carried it out into the hall and upstairs to a room where the little boy lay.

The sweet-faced lady was sitting by the bed, and as the nurse came in she held out her hand for the star.

"Is this what you wanted, my darling?" she asked, bending over the little boy.

The child nodded and held out his hands for the star, and as he clasped it a wonderful, shining smile came over his face. Then he fell asleep, holding the star tightly in one hand.

"Thank goodness," said the nurse. "I was worried for a while, but I'm sure now that he'll be fit and well again in no time."

And it was so. As long as the boy lived, he put the star on the very top of his

Christmas tree. And for the rest of the year, the golden star twinkled and spun on a string in the window, where it could look out at the great sky country.

Matthew Insists on Puffed Sleeves

An extract from *Anne of Green Gables*
by L M Montgomery

*Anne Shirley has been adopted by Marilla and her brother
Matthew. She has always longed for fashionable puffed sleeves,
but Marilla makes her dresses with plain sleeves.*

*M*atthew was having a bad ten minutes of it. He had come into the kitchen, in the twilight of a cold, grey December evening, and had sat down in the woodbox corner to take off his heavy boots, unconscious of the fact that Anne and a bevy of her schoolmates were having a practice in the sitting room. Presently they came trooping through the hall and out into the kitchen, laughing and chattering gaily. They did not see Matthew, who watched them shyly for ten minutes as they put on caps and jackets and talked about the concert.

Anne stood among them, as bright-eyed as they, but Matthew suddenly became conscious that there was something about her that was different from her mates. Anne had a brighter face, and bigger, starrier eyes, and more delicate features than the others. The difference that disturbed him did not consist in any of these respects. Then in what did it consist?

After two hours of hard reflection Matthew arrived at a solution to his problem. Anne was not dressed like the other girls!

The more Matthew thought about the matter the more he was convinced that Anne never had been dressed like the other girls – never since she had come to Green Gables. Marilla kept her clothed in plain, dark dresses, all made after the same unvarying pattern. Matthew was quite sure that Anne's sleeves did not look at all like the sleeves that the other girls wore. He recalled the cluster of little girls he had seen around her that evening and he wondered

why Marilla always kept Anne so plainly and soberly gowned.

Of course, it must be all right. Marilla knew best and Marilla was bringing her up. But surely it would do no harm to let the child have one pretty dress. Matthew decided that he would give her one. Christmas was only a fortnight off. A nice new dress would be the very thing for a present. Matthew, with a sigh of satisfaction, put away his pipe and went to bed, while Marilla opened all the doors and aired the house.

When Matthew came to think the matter over he decided that a woman was required to cope with the situation. Marilla was out of the question. Matthew felt sure she would throw cold water on his project at once. There remained only Mrs Lynde, for of no other woman in Avonlea would Matthew have dared to ask advice. To Mrs Lynde he went accordingly, and that good lady promptly took the matter out of the harassed man's hands.

"Pick out a dress for you to give Anne? To be sure I will. I'm going to Carmody tomorrow and I'll attend to it. Have you something particular in mind? No? Well, I'll just go by my own judgment then. I believe a nice rich brown would just suit Anne. Perhaps you'd like me to make it up for her, too, seeing that if Marilla was to make it Anne would probably get wind of it before the time and spoil the surprise? Well, I'll do it. I'll make it to fit my niece, Jenny Gillis, for she and Anne are as alike as two peas as far as figure goes."

"Well now, I'm much obliged," said

Matthew, "and – and – I dunno – but I'd like – I think they make the sleeves different nowadays to what they used to be. If it wouldn't be asking too much I – I'd like them made in the new way."

"Puffs? Of course. You needn't worry a speck more about it, Matthew. I'll make it up in the very latest fashion," Mrs Lynde said to him.

To herself she added when Matthew had gone, "It'll be a real satisfaction to see that poor child wearing something decent for once. The way Marilla dresses her is positively ridiculous, that's what, and I've ached to tell her so plainly a dozen times."

Marilla knew all the following fortnight that Matthew had something on his mind, but what it was she could not guess, until Christmas Eve, when Mrs Lynde brought

up the new dress.

"So this is what Matthew has been looking so mysterious over and grinning about to himself for two weeks, is it?" she said a little stiffly, but tolerantly. "I knew he was up to some foolishness. Well, I must say I don't think Anne needed any more dresses. I hope she'll be satisfied at last, for I know she's been hankering after those silly sleeves ever since they came in."

Christmas morning broke on a beautiful white world. It had been very mild, but just enough snow fell softly in the night to transfigure Avonlea. Anne peeped out from her frosted gable window with delighted eyes. The ploughed fields were stretches of snowy dimples, and there was a crisp tang in the air. She ran downstairs singing until her voice re-echoed through Green Gables.

CHRISTMAS IS COMING

"Merry Christmas, Marilla! Merry Christmas, Matthew! Isn't it a lovely Christmas? I'm so glad it's white. I don't like green Christmases. They're not green – they're just faded browns and greys. Why – Matthew, is that for me? Oh, Matthew!"

Matthew had sheepishly unfolded the dress from its paper swathings and held it out to her.

Anne took the dress and looked at it. Oh, how pretty it was – a lovely soft brown with all the gloss of silk, a skirt with dainty frills and a little ruffle of filmy lace at the neck. But the sleeves – they were the crowning glory! Long elbow cuffs, and above them two beautiful puffs divided bows of brown-silk ribbon.

"That's a Christmas present for you, Anne," said Matthew shyly. "Why – why –

don't you like it? Well now – well now."

For Anne's eyes had filled with tears.

"Like it! Oh, Matthew!" Anne laid the dress over a chair and clasped her hands. "Matthew, it's perfectly exquisite. Oh, I can never thank you enough. Look at those sleeves! Oh, it seems to me this must be a happy dream."

"Well, well, let us have breakfast," interrupted Marilla. "I must say, Anne, I don't think you needed the dress, but since Matthew has got it for you, see that you take good care of it. There's a hair ribbon Mrs Lynde left for you. It's brown, to match the dress. Come now, sit down."

"I don't see how I'm going to eat breakfast," said Anne rapturously. "Breakfast seems so commonplace at such an exciting moment. I'd rather feast my eyes on that

dress. It was lovely of Mrs Lynde to give me the ribbon too. I feel that I ought to be a very good girl indeed. I really will make an extra effort after this."

Cutting the Christmas Tree

An extract from *Peter and Polly in Winter*
by Rose Lucia

*Traditionally, in America, Christmas trees
were decorated with strings of popcorn.*

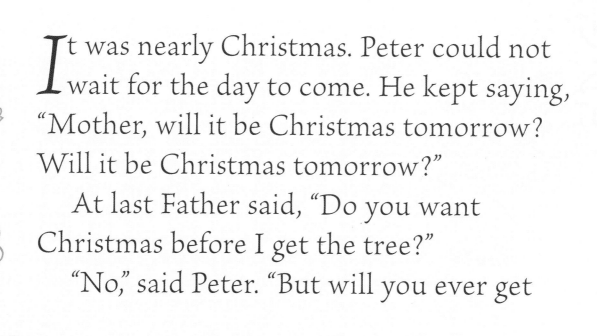

It was nearly Christmas. Peter could not wait for the day to come. He kept saying, "Mother, will it be Christmas tomorrow? Will it be Christmas tomorrow?"

At last Father said, "Do you want Christmas before I get the tree?"

"No," said Peter. "But will you ever get

the tree?"

"I will today. You and Polly may go with me. We will choose the prettiest fir tree we can find. Put on your things, and we will start now."

"Oh, goody, goody!" cried Peter, jumping up and down. "Now I know that Christmas is almost here."

"It will be here tomorrow," said Father. "Run and tell Polly."

They went through the field at the back of the house. They climbed over the stone-wall post office.

"We must find a strong tree, my boy. Can you see one you like?"

"That one," said Peter.

Father laughed. "That is a strong tree. But it is too tall. We should have to cut a hole in the ceiling to stand it up. Find a

smaller one."

"There is a good tree. See how pretty it is. It looks like our little firs at home."

"I believe that is just right for us, Polly. I will cut it down. Please hold my coat."

Father swung his axe. He gave three sharp blows. But all at once there was a chatter overhead.

In the next tree a grey squirrel was running up a large branch. He was scolding with all his might. His tail was jerking. He looked very cross.

"Well, old fellow," said Father, "did I disturb you? I am sorry. Go back to sleep. We will not take your tree."

"His is too bare, isn't it,

64

Father? The leaves have all gone. We must have a fir tree for ours. It has queer leaves. But they do not fall off in the winter."

"That is why we call such trees evergreens, Polly. They are always green. Pine trees are evergreens, too. Their needles are longer than fir needles."

Soon father had cut down the fir. He put it over his shoulder, and the end dragged on the snow.

"Now we are ready for home," he said. "Tonight Mother and I will dress this tree. Tomorrow you may see it."

"Have you really a dress for it?" asked Peter. "I hope it is red. Who made it?"

"O Peter, how silly you are! Father means dress it up with candy bags and popped corn and presents."

"I know now," said Peter. "Ponies and

guns and things."

"See the snow sparkle, children. The Sun makes it do that. Look at the blue sky. Doesn't the air feel good to you?"

"It makes me feel like running," said Polly, excitedly.

"Then run along, chicks. You will get home first. Tell Mother that the Christmas tree is really coming. You may pop the corn this afternoon."

When Peter and Polly got home, they ran into the house.

"Mother, Mother!" they shouted. "The Christmas tree is coming. Father has it."

"Why, Mother," said Polly, "what makes the house smell so sweet? For it smells just like the woods."

"It is the green wreaths, Polly. I have them in all the rooms. There is one on the

front door, too. These wreaths smell better than the ones that we buy. You may help me make the rest of them. We need more."

So the children went into the kitchen. On a table were pieces of evergreen boughs. They helped their mother twist the pieces into circles. On each circle she wound many small twigs. When done, the wreaths were firm and thick and green.

"How good it does smell, Mother. I like Christmas smells. But see my hands."

"That is the pitch from the greens, Polly. Just rub on a little butter. It will take off the pitch. Then wash your hands in warm water. I will clean up the rest of the greens. When this is done, we will pop our corn."

That was always fun. Polly liked to shake the popper. She liked to see the white kernels of corn hop up and down. She liked

the good smell, too.

Soon two large panfuls were popped. Then came another task. The corn must be strung. Polly and Peter both helped. But, of course, mother could string much faster than they. She told them stories while they worked.

"Now, children, the Giveaway Box is ready. You may choose your things to give away."

On the floor in the dining room there was a large box. It was filled with games, dolls, bags of candy and popped corn, and many other things.

These were for Peter and Polly to give away. They would make other children happy. And that would make Peter and

Polly happy, too.

Peter chose a jumping jack for Tim. Polly chose to give him a whistle.

"He cannot whistle with his mouth yet," Polly said. "But perhaps Collie will come for this whistle."

When Polly was out of the room, Peter chose a present for her. It was the prettiest doll that he had ever seen.

Polly chose a train of cars for Peter. But he did not know that.

"We could give this candlestick to Mrs White," said Polly. "I think she would like it."

Then Mother said, "Why don't you give the hot water bag to Grandmother? Her bag leaks."

"Oh, we will!" cried both children.

"There is my teacher," said Peter. "I will give her these marbles."

"Your teacher! You don't go to school, Peter," Polly said.

"I did one day," said Peter. "I like her. She was good to me. She is my teacher. I don't care what you say."

"Never mind about that, chicks," said Mother. "I'm afraid she hasn't a pocket for the marbles. Why don't you give her the box of handkerchiefs?"

Before long the Giveaway Box was empty. The presents were tied up. Every friend in the village had been remembered. Peter and Polly were tired. They were glad when it was bedtime.

As Mother tucked her up, Polly said, "I like the Giveaway Box. It is fun. It is as

much fun as it is to get things. You gave it to us, Mother. You give us everything."

"Father, too," said Mother. "And it makes fathers and mothers happy to do that."

Little Roger's Night in the Church

By Susan Coolidge

It was Christmas Eve. Little Roger sat in his grandparents' house eating his supper. Grandfather had gone to the church to put the fire in order for the night, lock up the doors and make all safe.

Suddenly Granny exclaimed, "Oh deary me! Grandfather has gone off and forgot his keys. Would you be afraid, little 'un, to run up with them?"

"Not a bit," said Roger. "I'll take 'em

down in a minute, and then run home."

So, after a goodnight hug from Granny, off he ran. The church was near, and the moon light as day, so he never thought of being afraid. Grandfather was stooping to cover the fire for the night. He was so busy he never knew Roger was there till he jingled the keys in his ear, but he laughed, well pleased.

"I only just missed them," he said. "You're a good boy to fetch them up. Are you going home with me tonight?"

"No, I'm to sleep at my mother's," said Roger, "but I'll wait and walk with you, Grandfather." So he slipped into a pew and sat down till the work should be finished, and as he looked up he saw all at once how beautiful the old church was looking.

The Moon outside was streaming in so

brightly that you hardly missed the Sun.
Roger could see all of the way up to the
carved beams of the roof, and trace the
figures on the great arched windows
over the altar.

To study the roof better,
Roger thought he would
lie flat on the cushion
awhile, and look
straight up. So he
arranged himself
comfortably, and
somehow – it will
happen even when
we are full of
enjoyment and
pleasure – his eyes shut. And the first
thing he knew he was rubbing them open
again, only a minute afterwards, as it

seemed. But Grandfather was gone. There was the stove closed for the night, and the great door was shut.

Roger jumped up in a fright, as you can imagine. He ran to the door and shook it hard. No – it was locked, and he was shut in for the night. He understood it all in a moment. The tall pew had hidden him from sight. Grandfather had thought him gone home. His mother would think that he was safe at the other cottage – no one would miss him, and there was no chance of being let out before morning.

Roger was only six years old, so no wonder that at first he felt frightened. But he was a brave lad, and that idea soon left him. He began to think that he was not badly off, after all, the church was warm, the pew cushion as soft as his bed. No one could get in to harm him. In fact, after the first moment, there was something so exciting and adventurous in the idea of spending the night in such a place, that he was almost glad the accident had happened. So he went back to the pew, and tried to go to sleep again.

Roger had heard the clock strike eleven a long time since. He was lying with eyes half shut, gazing at the red fire grate, and feeling at last a little drowsy, when all at once a strange rush seemed to come to him in the air, like a cool clear wind blowing through the church.

Just at this moment the church clock began to strike twelve. Roger listened to the deep notes – five – six – seven – eight – nine – ten – eleven – twelve. It was Christmas Day.

As the last echo died away, a new sound took its place. From far off came the babble of tiny voices drawing nearer. Then the church bells began to ring all together, a chime, a Christmas chime, only the sounds were as if baby hands had laid hold on the ropes. Almost before he knew it Roger was climbing the dark belfry stairs as fast as his feet could carry him.

Higher, higher – at last he gained the belfry. There hung the four great bells, but nobody was pulling at their heavy ropes.

On each iron tongue was perched a fairy, on the ropes clustered others, all swaying to and fro.

They floated in and out of the tower, they mounted the great bells and sat atop in swarms, they chased and pushed each other, playing all sorts of pranks.

How long the sight lasted Roger could not tell, but all at once there came a strain of music in the air, solemn and sweeter than ever mortal heard before. In a moment the fairies left their sports, flew from the tower in one sparkling drift, and were gone, leaving Roger alone.

And then he felt afraid, which he had

not been as long as the fairies were
there, and down he ran in a fright
and entered the church again.

The red glow of the fire was
good to feel, for he was shivering
with cold and excitement. But
hardly had he regained his old seat,
when a great marvel came to pass.

The wide window over the altar
swung open, and a train of angels
slowly floated through – Christmas
angels, with faces of calm, glorious beauty,
and robes as white as snow. Over the altar
they hovered, and a wonderful song rose
and filled the church. The words were few,
but again and again and again they came,
"Glory to God in the highest, and on Earth
peace, good will towards men."

Then the white-robed choir parted and

floated like soft summer clouds to and fro in the church, pausing here and there as in blessing. They touched the leaves of the Christmas greenery as they passed, they hung over the organ and brushed the keys with their wings, a long time they clustered above the benches, as if to leave a fragrance in the air, and, then noiseless as a cloud, they floated to the window. For one moment their figures could be seen against the sky, then the song died away – they were gone, and Roger saw them no more.

You can guess Grandfather's surprise when his little grandson ran to meet him with his wonderful story when he opened the church. He took the boy home to the cottage, and Granny speedily prepared a breakfast for her darling after his adventure. But Roger would go on telling of angels and fairies till both grandparents began to think him bewitched.

Perhaps he was, for to this day he persists in the story. And though the villagers that morning exclaimed that at no time had their old church looked so beautiful before, and though the organ sent forth a rarer, sweeter music than fingers had ever drawn from it, still nobody believed a word of it. "Roger had dreamed it all," they said.

I Saw Three Ships

Traditional

I saw three ships come sailing in,
On Christmas Day, on Christmas Day;
I saw three ships come sailing in,
On Christmas Day in the morning.

Pray, whither sailed those ships all three,
On Christmas Day, on Christmas Day;
Pray, whither sailed those ships all three,
On Christmas Day in the morning?

I Saw Three Ships

O they sailed into Bethlehem,
On Christmas Day, on Christmas Day;
O they sailed into Bethlehem,
On Christmas Day in the morning.

And all the bells on earth shall ring,
On Christmas Day, on Christmas Day;
And all the bells on earth shall ring,
On Christmas Day in the morning.

And all the angels in heaven shall sing,
On Christmas Day, on Christmas Day;
And all the angels in heaven shall sing,
On Christmas Day in the morning.

And all the souls on earth shall sing,
On Christmas Day, on Christmas Day;
And all the souls on earth shall sing,
On Christmas Day in the morning.

MAGICAL MOMENTS

The Nutcracker and the Mouse King

Adapted from a story
by Hoffmann

*Fritz and Marie have a godfather who
always brings them wonderful presents.*

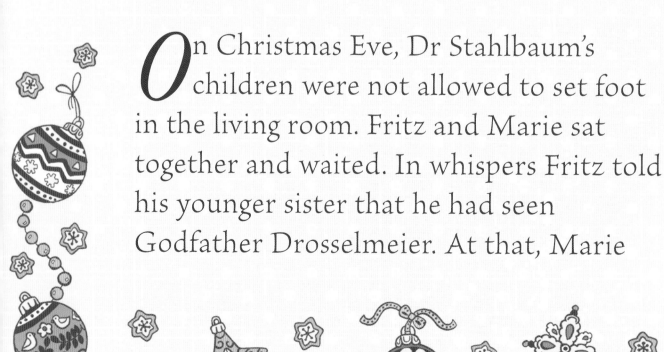

On Christmas Eve, Dr Stahlbaum's children were not allowed to set foot in the living room. Fritz and Marie sat together and waited. In whispers Fritz told his younger sister that he had seen Godfather Drosselmeier. At that, Marie clapped her hands and cried, "Oh, what do you think Godfather Drosselmeier has made for us?"

At that moment, a bell rang, the doors flew open and a flood of light streamed in.

"Come in children," said Papa and Mama.

The children stood silently with shining eyes. Then Marie found a silk dress hanging on the tree, and Fritz reviewed his new squadron of soldiers, who were fitted in red and gold uniforms.

Just then, the bell rang again. Knowing that Godfather Drosselmeier would be unveiling his present, the children ran to the table that had been set up beside the wall. The screen that had hidden it was taken away. Then the children saw a magnificent castle with dozens of sparkling windows and golden towers. Chimes played

as tiny ladies and gentlemen strolled around, and children in little skirts danced.

Fritz said, "Godfather Drosselmeier, let me go inside your castle."

"Impossible," said Mr Drosselmeier.

"Then I don't really care for it," said Fritz. "My squadron of soldiers are not shut up in a house."

Marie did not want to leave the Christmas table as she had just caught sight of something. When Fritz marched away, Marie noticed a little wooden man.

"Oh, Father dear," Marie cried out, "who does the dear little man belong to?"

"Dear child," said Dr Stahlbaum, "he belongs to us. He will crack hard nuts for you with his teeth."

Dr Stahlbaum lifted his wooden cloak, and the little man opened his mouth wide.

Marie put in a nut and – *crack* – the little man bit it in two, the shell fell down and Marie found the kernel in her hand.

Fritz ran over to his sister. He chose the biggest nut, and all of a sudden – *crack, crack* – three little teeth fell out of the Nutcracker's mouth.

"Oh, my poor little Nutcracker!" Marie cried.

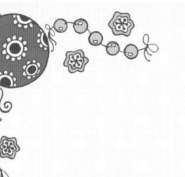

MAGICAL MOMENTS

"He's just a stupid fool," said Fritz. "He calls himself a nutcracker, and his teeth are no good."

"No, no!" Marie cried. "He's my dear Nutcracker." Sobbing, Marie wrapped the little man in her handkerchief.

Marie's mother put out all of the candles, leaving on only one lamp. "Go to bed soon," she said, "or you won't be able to get up tomorrow."

As soon as Marie was alone, she looked at the Nutcracker.

"Dear Nutcracker," she said softly. "I'm going to take care of you until you're well and happy again."

Marie placed him next to the other toys in a glass cabinet in the living room. She shut the door and was going to her bedroom, when she heard whispering and

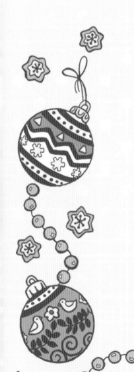

shuffling. The clock whirred twelve times. Then she heard giggling and squeaking all around her, followed by the sound of a thousand little feet scampering behind the walls. Soon Marie saw mice all over the room, and in the end they formed ranks.

At the same time, Marie saw a strange glow inside the toy cabinet. All at once, Nutcracker jumped from the cabinet.

"Trusty Drummer," cried the Nutcracker, "sound the advance!"

All the boxes containing Fritz's army burst open. Soldiers climbed out and jumped to the bottom shelf. Then they formed ranks on the floor.

A few moments later, guns were going *boom! boom!* The mice advanced and overran some of the artillery positions. Both sides fought with grim determination,

and for a long while victory hung in the balance. But then the mice brought up more troops.

The Nutcracker was in dire peril. He tried to jump over the ledge of the toy cabinet, but his legs were too short.

At that moment, the Mouse King charged the Nutcracker. Without quite knowing what she was doing, Marie took off her left shoe and flung it with all her might. At that moment, everything vanished from Marie's sight. She fell to the floor in a faint.

When Marie awoke from her deep sleep, she was lying in her own little bed.

"Oh, Mother dear," Marie whispered. "Have all the nasty mice gone away? Was the Nutcracker saved?"

"Don't talk such nonsense, child," said her mother. "What have mice got to do with the Nutcracker? "

"Oh, Mother," Marie broke in. "There was a big battle between the dolls and the mice. The mice were going to capture the Nutcracker. So I threw my shoe at the mice,

and after that I don't know what happened."

Then Godfather Drosselmeier came to visit. "I've brought you something," he told Marie. He reached into his pocket and took out the Nutcracker, who he had fixed as good as new. Marie cried out for joy!

That night, Marie was awakened in the moonlight by a strange rumbling. Then she saw the Mouse King squeeze through the hole in the wall. He jumped onto the table beside Marie's bed.

"Give me your candy," he said, "or I'll bite your Nutcracker to pieces." Then he slipped back into the hole.

Marie was so frightened that she could hardly say a word. That night she put her whole supply of sweet things at the foot of the toy cabinet. The next morning the candy was gone.

Marie was happy because she had saved the Nutcracker, but that night the Mouse King returned.

"Give me your beautiful dress and all your picture books," he hissed.

The next morning Marie went to the toy cabinet sobbing, and said to the Nutcracker, "Oh dear, what can I do? If I give that horrid Mouse King all my books and my dress, he'll just keep asking for more."

The Nutcracker said in a strained whisper, "Just get me a sword." At that his words ebbed away, and his eyes became fixed.

Marie asked Fritz for a sword, and Fritz slung it around the Nutcracker's waist.

The next night at the stroke of twelve, Marie heard clanging and crashing in the parlour. And then suddenly she heard a loud *Squeak!*

Soon Marie heard a soft knocking at the door and a faint little voice.

"Miss Stahlbaum, open the door and have no fear. I bring good news!"

Marie swiftly opened the door and found that the Nutcracker had turned into a prince!

The prince took Marie's hand and told her how he was really Godfather Drosselmeier's nephew, and an evil spell had turned him into a nutcracker. He said that when he defeated the Mouse King, the spell was broken and he was turned back into a prince.

Marie fell to the floor. When she opened

her eyes, she was lying in her little bed, and her mother was standing there.

"How can anyone sleep so long!" her mother exclaimed.

One day Marie's mother came into her room and said, "Your godfather's nephew from Nuremberg is here. So be sure to be on your best behaviour."

Marie turned as red as a beetroot when she saw the young man.

He went down on one knee and said, "Miss Stahlbaum, you see at your feet the happiest of men, whose life you saved on this very spot. Please come and reign with me over Marzipan Castle."

Marie said softly, "Of course I will come with you."

Then she left in a golden carriage.

And Marie is still the queen of a country

where the most wonderful things can be seen, as long as you have the right sort of eyes for it.

Christmas
Every Day

By William Dean Howells

Once there was a little girl who liked
Christmas so much that she wanted it
to be Christmas every day of the year. And
as soon as Thanksgiving was over, she began
to send postcards to
the old Christmas
Fairy to ask if she
might have her wish.
But the old Fairy
never answered. So

then she began to send her letters.

The day before Christmas she got a letter from the Fairy, saying she might have it Christmas every day for a year, and then they would see about having it longer. The little girl was a good deal excited already, preparing for the old-fashioned, once-a-year Christmas that was coming the next day, and perhaps the Fairy's promise didn't make such an impression on her as it would have made at some other time.

She went to bed early, so as to let Santa Claus have a chance at the stockings. In the morning she was up the first of anybody, and found hers all lumpy with packages of candy and oranges and rubber balls, and all kinds of small presents. Then she waited around till the rest of the family were up, and she was the first to burst into the

library, when the doors were opened, and look at the large presents laid out on the table – books, and boxes of stationery, and dolls, and little stoves, and skates, and snow shovels, and photograph frames, and boxes of watercolours, and nougat, and candied cherries, and dolls' houses – and the big Christmas tree, lighted and standing in a waste basket in the middle.

She had a splendid Christmas all day. She ate so much candy that she did not want any breakfast. Then she went round giving the presents she had got for other people, and came home and ate turkey and cranberry for dinner, and plum pudding and nuts and raisins and oranges and more candy. And then she went out and sledged, and came in with a stomach ache. They had a light supper, and pretty early everybody

went to bed cross.

The little girl slept very heavily, and she slept very late, but she was wakened at last by the other children dancing round her bed, with their stockings full of presents in their hands.

Christmas Every Day

"What is it?" said the little girl, and she rubbed her eyes.

"Christmas! Christmas! Christmas!" they all shouted.

"Nonsense! It was Christmas yesterday."

Her brothers and sisters just laughed. "We don't know about that. It's Christmas today, anyway."

Then all at once it flashed on the little girl that the Fairy was keeping her promise, and her year of Christmases was beginning. She was dreadfully sleepy, but she sprang up like a lark – a lark that had overeaten and gone to bed cross – and darted into the library. There it was again! Books, and boxes of stationery, and the rest, and there was the Christmas tree blazing away, and the family picking out their presents, but looking pretty sleepy. Her father was

perfectly puzzled, and her mother ready to cry. Her father said it seemed to him they had something just like it the day before, but he supposed he must have dreamt it.

Well, the next day, it was just the same thing all over again, but everybody was getting crosser. The little girl began to get frightened, keeping the secret all to herself. She wanted to tell her mother, but she didn't dare to. And she was ashamed to ask the Fairy to take back her gift, it seemed ungrateful, but she hardly knew how she could stand it, for a whole year.

So it went on and on, and it was Christmas on St Valentine's Day and Washington's Birthday, just the same as any day, and it didn't skip even the First of April, though everything was a trick that day, and that was some little relief.

After a while, turkeys got to be about a thousand dollars apiece, and cranberries – well, they asked a diamond apiece for cranberries. All the woods and orchards were cut down for Christmas trees, and after a while they had to make Christmas trees out of rags. But there were plenty of rags, because people got so poor, buying presents, that they couldn't get any new clothes, and they just wore their old ones to tatters.

Well, after it had gone on for about three or four months, the little girl, whenever she came into the room in the morning and saw

those great ugly, lumpy stockings dangling at the fireplace, and the disgusting presents around everywhere, used to just sit down and burst out crying. In six months she was perfectly exhausted – she couldn't even cry anymore. About the beginning of October she was sitting down on dolls wherever she found them, and by Thanksgiving she was throwing her presents across the room.

By that time people didn't carry presents around nicely any more. They flung them over the fence or through the window. And, instead of taking great pains to write 'For dear Papa,' or 'Jimmie,' or 'Jennie,' or whoever it was, they used to write, 'Take it, you horrid old thing!' and then go and bang it against the front door.

Nearly everybody had built barns to hold their presents, but pretty soon the

barns overflowed, and then they used to let them lie out in the rain, or anywhere.

Sometimes the police used to come and tell people to shovel their presents off the sidewalk, or they would arrest them.

Well, before Thanksgiving it had leaked

out who had caused all these Christmases. The little girl had suffered so much that she had talked about it in her sleep, and after that hardly anybody would play with her.

The very next day the little girl began to send letters to the Christmas Fairy to stop it. But it didn't do any good, so it went on till it came to the old, once-a-year Christmas Eve. The little girl fell asleep, and when she woke up in the morning she found that it wasn't Christmas at last, and wasn't ever going to be any more.

Well, there was the greatest rejoicing all over the country. The people met together everywhere, and kissed and cried for joy. The city carts went around and gathered up all the candy, and dumped them into the river. And the whole United States was one blaze of bonfires, where the children were

burning up their gift books and presents of all kinds. They had the greatest time!

The little girl went to thank the old Fairy because she had stopped it being Christmas, and she said she hoped the Fairy would see that Christmas never, never came again. Then the Fairy frowned and asked her if she was sure. This made the little girl think, and she said she would be willing to have it Christmas about once in a thousand years, and then she said a hundred, and then she said ten, and at last she got down to one. The Fairy said that was the good old way that had pleased people ever since Christmas began, and she was agreed.

Then the little girl said, "What're your shoes made of?"

The Fairy said, "Leather."

And the little girl said, "Bargain's done forever," and skipped off, and hippity-hopped the whole way home, she was just so glad.

Jimmy Scarecrow's Christmas

By Mary E Wilkins Freeman

Jimmy Scarecrow led a sad life in the winter. He liked to be useful, and in winter he was absolutely of no use at all. Every morning, when the wintry Sun peered across the dry corn stubble, Jimmy felt sad, but at Christmas time his heart nearly broke.

On Christmas Eve, Santa Claus came in his sledge, heaped high with presents. He was on his way to the farmhouse where

MAGICAL MOMENTS

Betsey lived with her Aunt Hannah.

Santa Claus had a large doll baby for her on his arm, tucked up against the fur collar of his coat. When poor Jimmy Scarecrow saw him, his heart gave a great leap.

"Santa Claus, please give me a little present. I was good all summer and kept the crows out of the corn," pleaded the poor scarecrow, but Santa Claus passed by.

The next morning, Betsey sat at the window holding her doll baby, and she looked out at Jimmy Scarecrow standing alone in the field amidst the corn stubble.

"Aunt Hannah?" she said.

"Well?" Aunt Hannah said. She was making a crazy patchwork quilt.

"Did Santa Claus bring the scarecrow a Christmas present?"

"No, of course he didn't."

"Why not?"

"Because he's a scarecrow. Don't ask such silly questions."

"I wouldn't like to be treated so, if I was a scarecrow," said Betsey.

It was snowing hard out of doors. The scarecrow's poor old coat got whiter and whiter. Aunt Hannah worked until the middle of the afternoon on her crazy quilt. Then she got up and spread it out over the sofa with an air of pride.

"There," she said, "that's done. I've got one for every bed in the house, and I've given four away. I'd give this away if I knew of anybody that wanted it."

Aunt Hannah put on her shawl and set out to visit her sister, who lived down the road. Half an hour after Aunt Hannah had gone, Betsey put her little red shawl over

her head, and ran across the field to Jimmy Scarecrow. She carried her new doll baby snuggled up under her shawl.

"Merry Christmas!" she said to Jimmy Scarecrow.

"Wish you the same," said Jimmy.

Betsey looked at the old hat fringed with icicles, and the old snow-laden coat.

"I've brought you a Christmas present," she said, and with that she tucked her doll baby inside Jimmy Scarecrow's old coat.

Jimmy Scarecrow's Christmas

"Thank you," said Jimmy Scarecrow.

"You're welcome," she said. "Keep her under your coat, so the snow won't wet her."

"Yes, I will," said Jimmy Scarecrow.

"Don't you feel cold in that old summer coat?" asked Betsey.

"If I had a little exercise, I should be warm," he replied. But he shivered, and the wind whistled through his rags.

"You wait a minute," said Betsey, and then she was off across the field.

Jimmy Scarecrow stood in the corn stubble, and soon Betsey was back again with Aunt Hannah's crazy quilt.

"Here," she said, "here is something to keep you warm," and she folded the crazy quilt around the scarecrow.

"Aunt Hannah wants to give it away if anybody wants it," she said. "Goodbye." And

with that she ran cross the field, and left Jimmy Scarecrow alone with the crazy quilt and the doll baby.

Jimmy Scarecrow had never felt so happy in his life as he did for an hour or so. But after that the snow began to turn to rain, and the crazy quilt was soaked through and through. And not only that, but so was his coat and the poor doll baby.

Suddenly he again heard Santa Claus' sleigh bells.

"Santa Claus! Dear Santa Claus!" cried Jimmy Scarecrow, and this time Santa Claus heard him.

"Who's there?" Santa Claus shouted out of the darkness.

Jimmy Scarecrow's Christmas

"Jimmy Scarecrow!"

Santa Claus got out of his sledge. "Have you been standing here ever since corn was ripe?" he asked pityingly, and Jimmy replied that he had.

"What's that over your shoulders?" Santa Claus continued.

"It's a crazy quilt."

"And what's that you're holding under your coat?"

"The doll baby that Betsey gave to me, and I'm afraid it's dead," poor Jimmy Scarecrow sobbed.

"Nonsense!" cried Santa Claus. "Let me see it!" And with that he pulled the doll baby out from under the scarecrow's coat, and patted its back, and it began to cry.

"It's all right," said Santa Claus. "Now get into the sledge, Jimmy Scarecrow, and come

with me to the North Pole!" he cried.

"Please, how long shall I stay?" asked Jimmy Scarecrow.

"Why, you are going to live with me," replied Santa Claus. "I've been looking for a person like you for a long time."

"Are there any crows to scare away at the North Pole?" Jimmy Scarecrow asked.

"No," answered Santa Claus, "I want you to scare away Arctic explorers from the North Pole. That is much more important than scaring away crows from corn. Come along – I am in a hurry."

"I will go on two conditions," said Jimmy. "First, I want to make a present for Aunt Hannah and Betsey, next Christmas."

"You shall make them any present you choose. What else?"

"I want some way provided to scare the

crows out of the corn next summer," said Jimmy Scarecrow.

"That is easily managed," said Santa Claus. "Just wait a minute."

Santa went with his lantern close to one of the fence posts and wrote these words upon it in crow language:

NOTICE
TO CROWS
Whichever crow shall hop or fly into this field during the absence of Jimmy Scarecrow shall be instantly turned snow-white, and be ever after a disgrace to his whole race:
Per order of Santa Claus.

MAGICAL MOMENTS

"The corn will be safe now," said Santa Claus. "Get in."

Jimmy got into the sledge and they flew away over the fields.

The next morning there was much surprise at the farmhouse, when Aunt Hannah and Betsey looked out of the window and the scarecrow was gone, and the crazy quilt and the doll baby with him.

"We'll have to have another scarecrow next summer," said Aunt Hannah.

But the next summer there was no need of a scarecrow, for not a single grain was stolen by a crow.

"It is a great mystery to me why the crows don't come into our cornfield," said Aunt Hannah.

But she had a still greater mystery to solve when Christmas came round again.

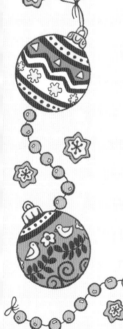

Jimmy Scarecrow's Christmas

She and Betsey each found a strange present in the sitting room on Christmas morning. Aunt Hannah's present was her old crazy quilt, remodelled, with every piece cut square and true, and matched exactly to its neighbour. Betsey's present was her doll baby of the Christmas before, but the doll was a year older. She had grown an inch, and could walk, and say, "Mamma," and "How do you do?"

Neither Aunt Hannah nor Betsey knew that the quilt and the doll were Jimmy Scarecrow's Christmas presents to them.

How Johnny Cricket Saw Santa Claus

An extract from *Friendly Fairies*
by Johnny Gruelle

When the first frost came and coated the leaves with its film of sparkles, Mamma Cricket, Papa Cricket, Johnny Cricket and Grandpa Cricket decided it was time to move into their winter home.

Papa, Mamma and Grandpa Cricket carried all the heavy cricket furniture, while Johnny Cricket carried the lighter things, such as the family portraits, looking glasses, knives and forks and spoons, and his own little violin.

Aunt Katy Didd wheeled Johnny's little sister Teeny in the cricket baby buggy, and helped Mamma Cricket lay the rugs and wash the stonework. For the Crickets' winter home was in the chimney of a big old-fashioned house, and the walls were very dusty and everything was topsy-turvy.

But Mamma Cricket and Aunt Katy Didd soon had everything in tip-top order, and the winter home was just as clean and neat as the summer home out under the rose bush had been.

There the Cricket family lived happily, and everything was just as cosy as any little bug would care to have. On cold nights the people who owned the great big old-fashioned house always made a fire in the

fireplace, so the walls of the Crickets' winter home were nice and warm. Little Teeny Cricket could play on the floor in her bare feet without fear of catching cold and getting the cricket croup.

There was one crack in the walls of the Crickets' winter home that opened right into the fireplace, so the light from the fire always lit up the Crickets' living room. Papa Cricket could read the *Bugville News*, while Johnny Cricket fiddled all the latest popular bug songs, and Mamma Cricket rocked and sang to Teeny Cricket.

One night, though, the people who owned the great big old-fashioned house did not have a fire in the fireplace. Little Teeny Cricket was bundled up in warm covers and rocked to sleep, and all the Cricket family went to bed in the dark.

How Johnny Cricket Saw Santa Claus

Johnny Cricket had just dozed into dreamland when he was awakened by something pounding ever so loudly. He slipped out of bed and into his two little red boots, and felt his way to the crack in the living room wall.

Johnny heard loud voices and merry peals of laughter, so he crawled through the crack and looked out into the fireplace.

There in front of the fireplace he saw four pink feet and two laughing faces way above, while just a couple of cricket hops from Johnny's nose was a great big man.

Then there were a few more squeals of laughter, and the four pink feet pitter-patted across the floor, and Johnny could see the owners hop into a snow-white bed.

Johnny saw the man walk to the lamp and turn the light down low, then leave the great big room.

Johnny Cricket jumped out of the crack into the fireplace, and ran out into the great big room. The light from the lamp was too dim for him to make out the objects hanging from the mantel above the fireplace. All he could see were four long black things.

So Johnny Cricket climbed up the bricks at the side of the fireplace until he came to the mantel shelf, then he ran along the shelf and looked over. He saw that the black things were stockings.

How Johnny Cricket Saw Santa Claus

Johnny began to wish that he had stopped to put on his stockings, for he had bare feet. He had removed his little red boots when he decided to climb up the side of the fireplace, and now his little feet were very cold.

So Johnny Cricket started to climb over the mantel shelf and down the side of the fireplace. And then suddenly there came a great puff of wind down the chimney that made the stockings swing away out into the room, and snowflakes fluttered clear across the room.

There was a tiny tinkle from a bell and, just as Johnny hopped behind the clock, he saw a boot stick out of the fireplace.

Then Johnny Cricket's little bug heart went *pitty-pat,* and sounded as if it would run a race with the ticking of the clock.

From his hiding place, Johnny Cricket heard one or two chuckles, and something rattle. He crept along the edge of the clock and, holding the two feelers over his back, looked from his hiding place.

At first all he could see were two hands filling the stockings with rattly things, but when the hands went down below the mantel for more rattly things, Johnny Cricket saw a big round smiling face, all fringed with snow-white whiskers.

Johnny drew back into the shadow of the clock and stayed there until all had grown quiet. Then he slipped from behind the clock and climbed down the side of the fireplace as fast as he could. Johnny Cricket was too cold to stop and put on his little red boots, but scrambled through the crack in the fireplace and hopped into bed.

In the morning, Mamma Cricket had a hard time getting Johnny out of bed. He yawned and stretched, put on one stocking, rubbed his eyes, yawned, put on another stocking and yawned again. He was still very sleepy and could hardly keep his eyes open as he reached for his little red boots.

Johnny's toe struck something hard, he yawned, rubbed his eyes and looked into the boot. Yes, there was something in Johnny Cricket's boot! He picked up the other boot. It, too, had something in it!

It was candy!

How Johnny Cricket Saw Santa Claus

With a loud cry for such a little cricket, Johnny rushed to the kitchen and showed Mamma Cricket.

And then Johnny Cricket told Mamma Cricket all about his exciting adventure the night before.

Mamma Cricket called Papa Cricket and they both had a laugh when Johnny told how startled he had been at the old man with the white whiskers who filled the stockings in front of the fireplace.

"Why, Johnny!" said Mamma and Papa Cricket. "Don't you know? That was Santa Claus. We have watched him every Christmas for the last four years fill the stockings. Santa Claus saw your little red boots and filled them with candy, too. If you crawl through the crack into the fireplace you will see the children of the

people who own this big house playing with all the presents that Santa Claus left them." And, sure enough, it was so.

Santa Claus' Helpers

An extract from *The Life and Adventures of Santa Claus*
by L Frank Baum

*In this story about Santa Claus, he has four magical
helpers called Kilter, Peter, Nuter and Wisk.*

One Christmas Eve, when his reindeer had leapt to the top of a new building, Santa Claus was surprised to find that the chimney had been built much smaller than usual. But he had no time to think about it just then, so he drew in his breath and made himself as small as possible, and slid

down the chimney.

'I ought to be at the bottom by this time,' he thought, as he continued to slip downwards. But no fireplace of any sort met Santa Claus' view, and by and by he reached the very end of the chimney, which was in the cellar.

"This is odd!" he reflected, much puzzled by the experience. "If there is no fireplace, what on earth is the chimney good for?"

Then he began to climb out again and found it hard work – the space being so small. And on Santa

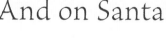

Santa Claus' Helpers

Claus' way up he noticed a thin, round pipe sticking through the side of the chimney, but he could not guess what it was for.

Finally he reached the roof and said to the reindeer, "There was no need of my going down that chimney, for I could find no fireplace through which to enter the house. I fear the children who live there must go without playthings this Christmas."

Santa Claus had not then discovered that stoves had been invented and were fast coming into use.

The following year Santa Claus found more and more of the new-fashioned chimneys that had no fireplaces, and the next year still more. The third year, so numerous had the narrow chimneys become, he even had a few toys left in his sledge that he was unable to give away,

because he could not get to the children.

The matter had now become so serious that it worried the good man greatly, and he decided to talk it over with Kilter, Peter, Nuter and Wisk.

Kilter already knew something about it. It had been his duty to run around to all the houses, just before Christmas, and gather up the notes and letters to Santa Claus that the children had written, telling him what they wished to be put in their stockings or hung on their Christmas trees.

"Well," declared the laughing Wisk, "we must abandon any thought of using these new-fashioned chimneys, but become burglars, and break into the houses some other way."

"What way?" asked Santa Claus.

"Why, walls of brick and wood and

plaster are nothing to fairies," said Wisk. "I can easily pass through them whenever I wish, and so can Peter and Nuter and Kilter. Is it not so, comrades?"

"I often pass through the walls when I gather up the letters," said Kilter.

"Therefore," continued the fairy, "you may as well take us with you on your next journey. And when we come to one of those houses with stoves instead of fireplaces, we will distribute the toys to the children without the need of using a chimney."

"That seems to me a good plan," replied Santa Claus, well pleased at having solved the problem. "We will try it next year."

That was how the four helpers all rode in the sledge with their master the following Christmas Eve. And they had no trouble at all in entering the new-fashioned

houses and leaving toys for the children
that lived in them.

Taken all together, the trip was a
great success, and to this day the four
little helpers always accompany
Santa Claus on his yearly ride, and
help him to distribute his gifts.

Santa Claus' Helpers

And Santa Claus soon found that parents were really anxious he should visit their homes on Christmas Eve and leave presents for their children.

So, to lighten his task, which was fast becoming very difficult indeed, even with his four helpers, Santa Claus decided to ask the parents to assist him.

"Get your Christmas trees all ready for my coming," he said to them. "And then I shall be able to leave the presents without loss of time, and you can put them on the trees when I am gone."

And to others he said, "See that the children's stockings are hung up in readiness for my coming, and then I can fill them as quick as a wink."

And often, when parents were kind and good-natured, Santa Claus would simply

fling down his package of gifts and leave the fathers and mothers to fill the stockings after he had darted away in his sledge.

"I will make all loving parents my deputies," cried the jolly old fellow, "and they shall help me do my work. For in this way I shall save many precious minutes and no children need be neglected for lack of time to visit them."

Besides carrying around the big packs in his swift-flying sledge, Santa Claus began to send great heaps of toys to the toy shops, so that if parents wanted larger supplies for their children they could easily get them. And if any children were, by chance, missed by Santa Claus on his yearly rounds, they could go to the toy shops and get enough to make them happy and contented.

Perhaps you will now understand how,

in spite of the size of the world, Santa Claus is able to supply all the children with beautiful gifts. To be sure, the old gentleman is rarely seen these days. But it is not because he tries to keep out of sight, I assure you. You see, he is so busy all year making toys, and so hurried on that one night when he visits our homes with his packs, that he comes and goes among us like a flash. It is almost impossible to catch a glimpse of him.

And, although there are millions more children in the world than there used to be, Santa Claus has never been known to complain of their increasing numbers.

"The more the merrier!" he cries, with a jolly laugh. The only difference is that his little workmen have to make their busy fingers fly faster every year to satisfy.

MAGICAL MOMENTS

"In all this world there is nothing so beautiful as a happy child," says good old Santa Claus. And if he had his way the children would all be beautiful, for all would be happy.

Raggedy Andy's Smile

An extract from *Raggedy Andy Stories*
by Johnny Gruelle

aggedy Andy's smile was gone. Not
entirely, but enough so that it made
his face seem onesided. If one viewed
Raggedy Andy from the left side, one could
see his smile. However, if one looked at
Raggedy Andy from the right side, one
could not see his smile. So Raggedy Andy's
smile was gone.

It really was not Raggedy Andy's fault.
He felt just as happy and sunny as ever.

And perhaps he would not have known the difference had not the other dolls told him he had only one half of his smile left.

Nor was it Marcella's fault. How was she to know that Dickie would feed Raggedy Andy orange juice and take off most of his cheery smile?

And besides, taking off one half of Raggedy Andy's smile, the orange juice left a great brown stain upon his face.

Marcella was very sorry when she saw what Dickie had done. However, Dickie's only sorrow was that Raggedy Andy was taken from him, and he could not feed Raggedy Andy more orange juice.

Raggedy Andy's Smile

Marcella kissed Raggedy Andy more than she did the rest of the dolls that night. She hung up a tiny stocking for each of the dollies, and placed a tiny china dish for each of the penny dolls beside their little spool box bed. For, as you probably have guessed, it was Christmas Eve, and Marcella was hoping Santa Claus would see the tiny stockings and place something in them for each doll.

Then, when the house was very quiet, the French doll told Raggedy Andy that most of his smile was gone.

"Indeed!" said Raggedy Andy. "I can still feel it. It must be there."

"Oh, but it really is gone!" Uncle Clem said. "It was the orange juice."

"Well, I still feel just as happy," said Raggedy Andy, "so let's have a jolly game of

some sort! What shall it be?"

"Perhaps we had best try to wash your face," said practical Raggedy Ann. She always acted as a mother to the other dolls when they were alone.

"It will not do a bit of good," the French doll told Raggedy Ann. "For I remember I had orange juice spilled upon a nice white frock I had one time, and the stain would never come out."

"That is too bad," Henny, the Dutch doll, said. "We shall miss Raggedy Andy's cheery smile when he is looking straight at us."

"You will have to stand on my right side when you wish to see my smile!" said Raggedy Andy. "But I wish everyone to understand that I am smiling just the same, whether you can see it or not."

And with this, Raggedy Andy caught

hold of Uncle Clem and Henny, and made a dash for the nursery door, followed by all the other dolls.

Raggedy Andy intended jumping down the stairs, head over heels, for he knew that neither he, Uncle Clem nor Henny would break anything by jumping down stairs.

But just as they got almost to the door, they dropped to the floor in a heap, for there, standing watching the whole performance, was a man.

Raggedy Andy, Uncle Clem and Henny stopped so suddenly they fell over each other. Raggedy Andy, being in the lead and pulling the other two, slid right through the door and stopped at the feet of the man.

A cheery laugh greeted this, and a chubby hand reached down and picked up Raggedy Andy and turned him over.

MAGICAL MOMENTS

Raggedy Andy looked up into a cheery little round face, with a little red nose and red cheeks, and all framed in white whiskers that looked just like snow.

Then the little round man walked into the nursery, and picked up all the dolls and looked at them. He made no noise when he walked, and this was why he had taken the dolls by surprise at the head of the stairs.

The little man with the snow-white whiskers placed all the dolls in a row, and from a little case in his pocket he took a tiny bottle and a little brush. He dipped the little brush in the tiny bottle and touched all the dolls' faces with it.

He had purposely saved Raggedy Andy's face until last. Then, as all the dolls watched, the cheery little white-whiskered man touched Raggedy Andy's face with the

148

magic liquid. The orange juice stain disappeared, and in its place came Raggedy Andy's rosy cheeks and cheery smile.

And, turning Raggedy Andy so that he could face all the other dolls, the cheery little man showed him that all the other dolls had new rosy cheeks and newly painted faces. They all looked just like new dollies. Even Susan's cracked head had been made whole.

Henny, the Dutch doll, was so surprised he fell over backwards and said, "Squeak!"

Then the little man put something in each of the tiny doll stockings, and something in each of the tiny china dishes for the two penny dolls.

Then, as quietly as he had entered, he left. Raggedy Andy heard him chuckling to himself as he went down the stairs.

Raggedy Andy's Smile

Raggedy Andy tiptoed to the door and over to the head of the stairs. Then he motioned for the other dolls to come.

There, from the head of the stairs, they watched the cheery little white-whiskered man take pretty things from a large sack and place them about the chimneyplace.

'He does not know that we are watching him,' the dolls all thought to themselves.

MAGICAL MOMENTS

But when the little man had finished his task, he turned and laughed right up at the dolls, for, of course, he had known that they were watching him all the time.

Then the little man swung the sack over his shoulder, and with a whistle he was gone – up the chimney.

The dolls were very quiet as they walked back into the nursery and sat down to think it all over.

And as the dolls sat there thinking, they heard out in the night the distinct *tinkle, tinkle, tinkle* of tiny sleigh bells, growing fainter and fainter as they disappeared in the distance.

Without a word, the dolls all climbed into their beds, just as Marcella had left them, and they all pulled the covers up to their chins.

Raggedy Andy's Smile

And Raggedy Andy lay there, his little shoe button eyes looking straight towards the ceiling, and smiling a joyful smile – not a half smile this time, but a full-size smile.

A Visit from St Nicholas

By Clement Clarke Moore

'Twas the night before Christmas, when all through the house
Not a creature was stirring, not even a mouse;
The stockings were hung by the chimney with care,
In hopes that St Nicholas soon would be there.

The children were nestled all snug in their beds,
While visions of sugar-plums danced in their heads.
And mamma in her 'kerchief, and I in my cap,
Had just settled our brains for a long winter's nap.

A Visit from St Nicholas

When out on the lawn there arose such a clatter,

I sprang from the bed to see what was the matter.

Away to the window I flew like a flash,

Tore open the shutters and threw up the sash.

The moon on the breast of the new-fallen snow

Gave the lustre of midday to objects below.

When, what to my wondering eyes should appear,

But a miniature sleigh, and eight tiny reindeer.

With a little old driver, so lively and quick,

I knew in a moment it must be St Nick.

More rapid than eagles his coursers they came,

And he whistled, and shouted, and called them by name!

"Now, Dasher! Now, Dancer! Now, Prancer and Vixen!

On, Comet! On, Cupid! On, on Donner and Blitzen!

To the top of the porch! To the top of the wall!

Now dash away! Dash away! Dash away all!"

MAGICAL MOMENTS

As dry leaves that before the wild hurricane fly,
When they meet with an obstacle, mount to the sky.
So up to the house-top the coursers they flew,
With the sleigh full of toys, and St Nicholas too.

And then, in a twinkling, I heard on the roof
The prancing and pawing of each little hoof.
As I drew in my head, and was turning around,
Down the chimney St Nicholas came with a bound.

He was dressed all in fur, from his head to his foot,
And his clothes were all tarnished with ashes and soot.
A bundle of toys he had flung on his back,
And he looked like a peddler, just opening his pack.

His eyes – how they twinkled! His dimples how merry!
His cheeks were like roses, his nose like a cherry!
His droll little mouth was drawn up like a bow,
And the beard of his chin was as white as the snow.

A Visit from St Nicholas

The stump of a pipe he held tight in his teeth,
And the smoke it encircled his head like a wreath.
He had a broad face and a little round belly,
That shook when he laughed, like a bowlful of jelly!

He was chubby and plump, a right jolly old elf,
And I laughed when I saw him, in spite of myself!
A wink of his eye and a twist of his head,
Soon gave me to know I had nothing to dread.

He spoke not a word, but went straight to his work,
And filled all the stockings, then turned with a jerk.
And laying his finger aside of his nose,
And giving a nod, up the chimney he rose!

He sprang to his sleigh, to his team gave a whistle,
And away they all flew like the down of a thistle.
But I heard him exclaim, 'ere he drove out of sight,
"Happy Christmas to all, and to all a good night!"

WINTER WONDERLAND

Christmas Under the Snow

An extract from *Kristy's Queer Christmas*
by Olive Thorne Miller

Willie and his family live on the prairies.

It was just before Christmas, and Mr Barnes was starting for the nearest village. "Don't forget the Christmas dinner, Papa," said Willie.

"'Specially the chickens for the pie!" put in Nora.

"An' the waisins," piped up little Tot.

"I hate to have you go, George," said

Mrs Barnes, anxiously. "It looks to me like a storm. If there is a bad storm, stay in the village till it is over. We can get along alone for a few days, can't we, Willie?"

"Oh, yes! Papa, I can take care of Mamma," said Willie.

"Well, Willie, I depend on you to take care of Mamma, and to get a Christmas dinner, if I don't get back," were Papa's last words as the faithful old horse started.

Mrs Barnes looked to where a low, heavy bank of clouds was slowly rising, and went into the snug little log cabin.

"Willie," she said, "I'm sure there's going to be a storm. You had better prepare enough wood for two or three days."

"I wish the village was not so far off," said Willie, as he came in with his last load.

Mrs Barnes glanced out of the window.

Broad scattering snowflakes were silently falling. "So do I," she replied, anxiously, "or that Papa did not have to come over that dreadful prairie."

Supper was soon eaten and cleared away, the fire carefully covered up, and the whole little family quietly in bed. Then the storm came down upon them in earnest.

The bleak wind howled, the white flakes came with it in millions and millions, and hurled themselves upon that house. They piled up outside, covered the steps, and then the door, and then the windows, and then the roof, and at last buried it completely out of sight.

Christmas Under the Snow

The night passed away and morning came, but no light broke through the windows. Mrs Barnes woke at the usual time, but finding it still dark and perfectly quiet outside, she turned over to sleep again. At that moment the clock struck, and the truth flashed over her.

Being buried under snow is no uncommon thing on the wide prairies, and since they had wood and cornmeal in plenty, Mrs Barnes would not have been much alarmed if her husband had been home. But snow deep enough to bury them must cover up all landmarks, and she knew her husband would not rest till he had found them.

"Willie," she said, "are you awake?"

"Yes, Mamma," said Willie.

"Willie," said his mother quietly, "I think

– I'm afraid – we are snowed in. Light a candle and look out the window."

Willie drew back the curtain. Snow was tightly banked up against it to the top.

"Why, Mamma," he exclaimed, "How can Papa find us? And what shall we do?"

"We must do the best we can," she said.

Breakfast was taken by candlelight, dinner in the same way, and supper passed with no sound from the outside world.

It was hard to keep up the courage of the little household. Nora said that tonight was Christmas Eve, and no Christmas dinner was to be had.

A thought struck Willie that he was sure would cheer up the rest. He brought out of a corner of the attic an old boxtrap, set it carefully on the snow, and scattered crumbs of cornbread.

In half an hour he went up again, and found to his delight that he had caught a rabbit, which had come to find food.

The rabbit was quietly laid to rest, and the trap was set again. This time another rabbit was caught. This was the last of them, but the next catch was a couple of snowbirds. These Willie carefully placed in a corner of the attic, using the trap for a cage, and giving them plenty of food and water.

The snowbirds were to be Christmas presents for the girls, and the rabbits were to make a pie. As for plum pudding, of course that couldn't be thought of.

"But don't you think, Mamma," said Willie eagerly, when the girls were fast asleep, with tears on their cheeks for the dreadful Christmas they were going to have, "that you could make some sort of a cake, and wouldn't hickory nuts be good in it? You know I have some left up in the attic," he continued.

"Well, perhaps so," said Mamma. "If I only had some eggs – but I have heard that snow beaten into cake would make it light – and there's snow enough, I'm sure,"

Willie cracked the nuts then prepared the two rabbits, which were to be their Christmas dinner.

"Merry Christmas!" he called out to Nora and Tot when they woke in the morning. "See what Santa Claus has brought you!"

Before they had time to think, the girls each received their presents, a live bird, that was never to be kept in a cage, but would fly about the house till summer came, and then go away if it wished.

Pets were scarce on the prairie, and the girls were delighted. They thought no more of the dinner, but hurried to dress themselves and feed the birds, which were now quite tame from hunger.

But after a while they saw preparations for dinner, too. Mamma made a crust and lined a deep dish, then she brought something like chicken and put it in the dish with a crust, and set it to bake.

And that was not all.

Mamma got out some more cornmeal, and put in some sugar and the nuts, and then Willie brought her a cup of snow, which she beat into the cake, while the children laughed at the idea of making a cake out of snow. This went into the same oven and pretty soon the cake rose up light, while the pie was sending out the most delicious odours.

At the last minute, when the table was set and everything was ready, Willie ran to look out of the attic skylight. In a moment there came a wild shout down the ladder.

"It's Papa!"

"Willie!" a voice called back over the snow. "Is all well?"

"All well!" shouted Willie, "and just going to have our Christmas dinner."

"Dinner?" echoed Papa. "Where is the house, then?"

"Oh, down here!" called Willie, "under the snow."

"Well, my son," said Papa, once he had climbed into the house. "You did take care of Mamma, and get a dinner out of nothing, which I am sure is delicious."

So it proved to be – even the snow pudding, which was voted very nice. When they had finished, Mr Barnes added his Christmas presents to Willie's, but nothing was quite so nice in their eyes as the two live birds.

After dinner, Papa and Willie dug out passages through the snow. Then Willie made tunnels and little rooms under the

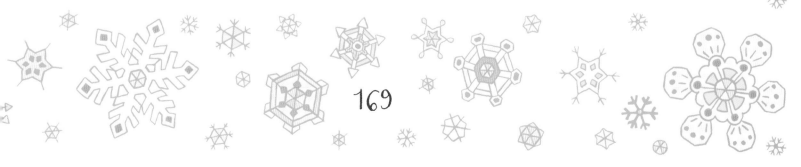

snow. And for two weeks, while the snow lasted, Nora and Tot had fine times in the little snow playhouses.

Jimmieboy's Snowman

By John Kendrick Bangs

*T*he snow had been falling fast for almost forty-eight hours, and Jimmieboy was almost crazy with delight. His father had made him a snowman with shoe buttons for eyes and a battered old hat on his head.

After the snowman was finished, Jimmieboy shouted in great glee for an hour or more, and then he ran up into his bedroom to rest.

After a while Jimmieboy ran to the window to see if the snowman was all right, and he was much surprised to discover that he wasn't there at all. The snowman couldn't have melted, that was certain, for the air was colder than it had been when the snowman was put up.

'It's strange!' thought Jimmieboy. 'He was there ten minutes ago.'

And then the doorbell rang, and Jimmieboy went to the door and opened it. There was the snowman!

"Won't you come in?" asked Jimmieboy.

The snowman stared at Jimmieboy and then said:

"Indeed, I'll enter not that door,
I've tried it once or twice before."

"Didn't you like it?" Jimmieboy asked.

"Oh, yes, I liked it well enough,
Although it used me pretty rough.
I lost a nose and foot and ear,
Last time I happened to come here."

"Do you always speak in rhyme?" asked Jimmieboy, surprised.

"Always, except when I speak in prose," said the snowman. "But say, don't stand there with the door open letting all the heat out into the world. If you want to talk to me, come outside."

"Very well," said Jimmieboy. "I'll come, if you'll wait until I bundle up a little so as to keep warm."

"All right, I'll wait," the snowman answered. "I'll take you up to where I live and introduce you to my boys if you like – only hurry. If a thaw should set in we might have trouble.

The snowman smiled happily as Jimmieboy came out, and then, taking him by the hand, the two of them went off up the road together.

"I'm glad you weren't offended with me because I wouldn't go in and sit down in your house," said the snowman. "I had a very narrow escape thirty winters ago, when I was young and didn't know any better. A small boy asked me to go into his house. I said all right, and in I went, never thinking that the house was hot and that I'd be in danger of melting away. The boy got out his picture books and we sat down before a blazing log fire. Suddenly the boy turned white as I was, and cried out, 'What have you done with your leg?'

"Would you believe it, Jimmieboy, that the minute I tried to rise and hop off on the search I discovered that my other leg was gone too?"

"How dreadful," Jimmieboy said.

"It was fearful," returned the snowman, "but that wasn't half. I raised my hand to my forehead when off dropped my right arm, and as I reached out with my left to pick it up again, that dropped off too. Then the boy cried out, 'Why, I know what's the matter. You are melting away!'

"He was right. Fortunately, as my neck began to go and my head rolled off the chair onto the floor, the boy picked it up – it was all that was left of me – and threw it

out of the window. If it hadn't been for that I should have met the horrid fate of my cousin the iceberg."

"What was that?" asked Jimmieboy.

"Oh, he wanted to travel," said the snowman, "so he floated off down to South America and woke up one morning to find himself nothing but a tankful of the Gulf of Mexico. We never saw him again."

"Do you live near here?" asked Jimmieboy, as he trudged along at the snowman's side.

"When summer comes I move up to the North Pole," replied the snowman.

Jimmieboy peered curiously along the road, at the far end of which he could see a huge mound of snow.

"Do you live in that?" he asked.

"Yes," the snowman replied. "The house

part of it is always as cold as ice – it's cooled by a special kind of refrigerator I had put in, which consumes about half a tonne of ice a week."

Jimmieboy laughed. "It's a cold furnace," he said.

"Precisely," answered the snowman. "Once in a while my boys run in the Sun and get warmed through, but I dose 'em up with ice water and cold cream and they soon get chilled again. But come, shall we go in now?"

By this time they had reached the side of the snowdrift, and Jimmieboy was pleased to see a door at one side of it. This the snowman opened, and they entered together a marvellously beautiful garden, glistening with frosty flowers and snow-clad trees. At the end of the garden was a little white house that looked like the icing on Jimmieboy's birthday cake. As they approached it, a dozen small-sized snow boys rushed out and began to pelt the snowman and Jimmieboy with snowballs.

"Hold up, boys," cried the snowman. "I've brought a friend home to see you."

The boys stopped at once, and Jimmieboy was introduced to them. They showed him wondrous snow toys, among which were rocking horses, railway trains and soldiers – all made of the same soft fleecy substance from which the snowman and his children were constructed.

When Jimmieboy had played for a long time with these, they gave him caramels and cream cakes, also made of snow.

After this the boys invited him out to sledge, and he went along with them. It

took his breath away the first time he went down, but when he got used to it he found the sport delightful. He was glad, however, when a voice from the little white house called to the children to return.

"Come in now, boys," it said. "It is getting too warm for you to stay out."

The snowman looked a little anxious, Jimmieboy thought, but he supposed this was because the littlest snow boy had overheated himself at his play, and had come in minus two fingers and an ear.

It was not this, however, that bothered him, as Jimmieboy found out in a few minutes. For the snowman simply restored the missing fingers and the ear by making a new lot for the little fellow out of a handful of snow he got in the garden. The real cause of his anxiety came out when the father of

this happy little family of snow boys called Jimmieboy to one side.

"You must go home right away," he said. "I'm sorry, but we have got to fly just as hard as we can or we are lost."

"But—" said Jimmieboy.

"Don't ask for reasons," returned the snowman, gathering his little snow boys together and rushing off with them. "Just read that and you'll see. Farewell."

Jimmieboy picked up the thing the snowman had told him to read. It was a newspaper. At the top was an announcement in huge letters:

WARM WEATHER TONIGHT

WISE SNOWMEN WILL MOVE NORTH AT ONCE

When Jimmieboy saw this he knew right away why he had been deserted. He walked to the front door and opened it, and what do you suppose it opened into?

It opened into Jimmieboy's bedroom, and when the door closed after him, lo and behold it wasn't there!

Nor was the snowman to be found the next morning. There wasn't even a sign of the shoe button eyes or the battered hat, as there certainly would have been had he melted instead of run away.

A Christmas Tree Adventure

An extract from *Captain Ted*
by Louis Pendleton

Everything was ready for Christmas at home – mince pies, fruit cake, a fat turkey hanging out in the cold – and no doubt the as yet mysteriously reserved presents would be plentiful and satisfactory. Only a tree was still needed, and Ted and Hubert were to get it.

So they tramped up the long hill at the back of the Ridgway farm towards the woods of evergreens and leafless maples.

The landscape as far as the eye could see was white with snow, but its depth, except in drifts, was only about two inches. Ted dragged a sled with rope to strap the tree on. Hubert trudged beside him carrying a heavy sharp hatchet.

"Aunt Mary said we must get a good one, small size, and I'm going to hunt till we do," said Ted.

About two-thirds of the way up the long white stretch of hillside, the boys paused on the brink of a pit that had been dug years before by a thick-witted settler in a hopeless quest for gold. The snows of the windy hillside had drifted into it until the bottom was deeply covered.

The boys paused to take a look into the big pit, and then continued on their way up the remaining stretch of open hillside. They explored the woods for a quarter of a mile or more before they found just the sort of gracefully branching spruce that they wanted. In no great while this was cut down, the spreading branches were roped in, and the trunk tied on the sled, which was then dragged out into the open.

The long descent towards the distant farmhouse was gradual enough to make sledding safe. Ted declared that the easiest way to get down with their load was to slide down, and Hubert agreed.

"But we'd better look out for the pit," added Hubert.

"Oh, we'll aim *so* as to leave that away to one side," said Ted confidently.

And so they did. After a running start, Ted leapt on the sled, straddling the trunk of the Christmas tree, and Hubert flung

himself with a shout onto the branches.

Away they went, shouting happily, now
quite forgetting the pit in their excitement.
They only laughed when they bumped into
a snow-covered obstruction and were
swerved to the left of their intended course.
They laughed again when another bump

carried them still further to the left. A third mishap of the same kind awoke Ted to the danger, but too late.

He had hardly begun to kick his heels into the snowy surface whirling past, in an effort to change their course, and to shout, "Look out!" in great alarm, when Hubert, whose view was obstructed by the branches of the spruce, became aware of a sudden silence and felt himself sinking through space. The younger boy scarcely realized that they had gone over the brink of the pit until he found himself floundering at the bottom in the snow, which happily was deep enough to break the force of their fall and save them from injury.

As soon as he found that neither Hubert nor himself had been harmed, Ted laughed over their struggles in snow up to their

waists, but Hubert thought it was no laughing matter.

"We certainly were fools to try it," admitted Ted. He floundered up to a higher level of the pit's bottom, where the snow was only about two feet deep, extended a hand to Hubert, and then pulled the tree-laden sled after them.

"Now, how are we going to get out?" he asked excitedly.

"We can't get out," said Hubert, looking around at the pit's steep sides.

"But we must, Hu. Anyhow, somebody's sure to come along."

But nobody did. They shouted again and again, as time passed, and listened in vain for an answer. Meanwhile Ted tried every means of escape he could think of. He first proposed to cut steps into the side of the

pit, but the hatchet could not be found. Hubert had either lost his grip on it as they were sledding down the hill, or it was now somewhere under the deep snow in the bottom of the pit.

Ted next proposed to throw the rope around a sapling that hung over the very brink some fifteen feet above their heads. He unstrapped the Christmas tree from the sled, coiled half the rope, and attempted to throw it over the sapling. Several times he succeeded in throwing the coil as high as the top of the pit, but always failed to throw it around the little tree.

"Oh, it's no use," groaned Hubert at last. "We'll never get out."

"Now, Hubert, you mustn't give up," urged Ted. "Boy Scouts don't give up. We'll get out somehow."

"But we'll have to stay here until tomorrow and we'll freeze to death. I'm nearly frozen now."

"Hubert, you quit that," rebuked Ted. "Jump up and down and swing your arms if you're cold, but don't do the baby act."

Hubert was silenced. He exercised his numb limbs, as advised, and watched Ted as he prepared to try out yet another plan. With his pocket knife, Ted picked stones out of the side of the pit until he found one he thought might serve his purpose – an oblong, jagged bit of rock around which the rope could be securely tied. Again and again Ted threw this stone – the rope trailing after it – without succeeding in sending it around the sapling.

The Sun had set and Hubert's teeth chattered, when, almost ready to give up, it occurred to Ted to toss the stone up with both hands and all his strength, aiming half a foot to the right of the leaning sapling. This carried the stone higher than it had gone before and, at the second trial, it struck the incline above the tree, rolled and came down on the other side, carrying the rope around the trunk and bringing it within reach of Ted's hand. He drew it down and tied the two ends together.

Within five minutes Ted had clambered out of the pit. Then Hubert began his struggle to follow, but Ted stopped him, insisting that both the sled and the Christmas tree be drawn out first. Then Hubert, with the rope tied round his waist, was hauled to the upper level after much effort and some strain on the part of both the boys.

"I'll never slide down that hill again," vowed Hubert, as they neared the cheeringly lit farmhouse, dragging the sled and tree.

But Ted only said, "I'm glad we managed

to get out without help."

As they were going to bed that night, Hubert said, "I can't wait till I see my Christmas presents!"

Making Angels in the Snow

An extract from *Raggedy Andy Stories*
by Johnny Gruelle

"Whee! It's good to be back home
again!" said Raggedy Andy to the
other dolls, as he stretched his feet out in
front of the little toy stove and rubbed his
rag hands briskly together, as if to warm
them through.

All the dolls laughed at Raggedy Andy
for doing this, for they knew there had
never been a fire in the little toy stove.

"We are so glad and happy to have you

back home again with us!" the dolls told
Raggedy Andy.

"Well," Raggedy Andy replied, as he held
his rag hands over the tiny lid of the stove
and rubbed them again, "I have missed all
of you and wished many times that you had
been with me."

And as Raggedy Andy continued to hold
his hands over the little stove, Uncle Clem
asked him why he did it.

Raggedy Andy smiled and leaned back in
his chair. "Really," he said, "I wasn't paying
any attention. I've spent so much of my
time while I was away drying out my soft
cotton stuffing it seems as though it has
almost become a habit."

"Were you wet most of the time,
Raggedy Andy?" the French doll asked.

"Nearly all the time." Raggedy Andy

replied. "First I would get sopping wet and then I'd freeze!"

"Freeze!" exclaimed all the dolls together in one breath.

"Dear me, yes!" Raggedy Andy laughed. "Just see here." And he pulled his sleeve up and showed the dolls where his rag arm had been mended. "That was quite a rip!"

The dolls gathered around Raggedy Andy and examined the rip in his rag arm.

"It's all right now," he laughed. "But you should have seen me when it happened! I was frozen into one solid cake of ice all the way through, and when Marcella tried to limber up my arm before it had thawed out, it went *Pop!* and just burst.

"Then I was placed in a pan of nice warm water until the icy cotton inside me had melted, and then I was hung up on a

196

line above the kitchen stove, out at Gran'ma's."

"But how did you happen to get so wet and then freeze?" asked Raggedy Ann.

"Out across the road from Gran'ma's home, way out in the country, there is a lovely pond," Raggedy Andy explained. "When Marcella and I went out to Gran'ma's, last week, Gran'ma met us with a sleigh, for the ground was covered with starry snow. The pretty pond was covered with ice, too, and upon the ice was a soft blanket of the white, white snow. It was beautiful!" said Raggedy Andy.

"Gran'ma had a lovely new sled for Marcella, a red one with shiny runners.

"It was heaps of fun, for there was a little

hill at one end of the pond, so that when we coasted down, we went scooting across the pond like an arrow.

"Marcella would turn the sled sideways, just for fun, and she and I would fall off and go sliding across the ice upon our backs. Then Marcella showed me how to make angels in the soft snow!"

"Oh, tell us how, Raggedy Andy!" shouted all the dollies.

"It's very easy," said Raggedy Andy. "Marcella would lie down upon her back in the snow and put her hands back up over her head, then she would bring her hands in a circle down to her sides, like this." And Raggedy Andy lay upon the floor of the nursery and showed the dollies just how it was done. "Then," he added, "when she stood up it would leave the print of her

body and legs in the white, white snow, and
where she had swooped her arms there
were the angel's wings!"

"It must have looked just like an angel!"
said Uncle Clem.

"Indeed it was very pretty!" Raggedy Andy answered. "Then Marcella made a lot of angels by placing me in the snow and working my arms. So you see, what with falling off the sled so much and making so many angels, Marcella and I were both wet, but I was completely soaked through. My cotton just became soppy and I was ever so much heavier!

"Just as we were having a most delightful time, Gran'ma came to the door and 'Ooh-hooed' to Marcella to come and get a nice new doughnut. So Marcella, thinking to return in a minute, left me lying upon the sled and ran through the snow to Gran'ma's. And there I stayed until I began to feel stiff, and I could feel the cotton inside me begin to freeze.

"I lay upon the sled until after the Sun

went down. After it had been dark for some time, I heard someone coming through the snow and could see the yellow light of a lantern. It was Gran'ma.

"She pulled the sled over and then she picked me up and took me inside. 'He's frozen as stiff as a board!' she told Marcella as she handed me to her. Marcella did not say why she had forgotten to come for me, but I found out afterwards that it was because she was so wet. Gran'ma made her change her clothes and shoes, and would not permit her to go out and play again.

"Well, anyway," concluded Raggedy Andy. "That is the way it went all the time we were out at Gran'ma's – I was wet nearly all the time. But I wish you could all have been with me to share in the fun."

Raggedy Andy again leaned over the

little toy stove and rubbed his rag hands briskly together.

Uncle Clem went to the waste paper basket and came back with some scraps of yellow and red paper. Then, taking off one of the tiny lids, he stuffed the paper in part of the way, as if flames were shooting up!

Then, as all the dolls' merry laughter rang out, Raggedy Andy stopped rubbing his hands, and catching Raggedy Ann about the waist, he went skipping across the nursery floor with her, whirling so fast neither saw they had gone out through the door until it was too late. For coming to the head of the stairs, they both went head over heels, *blumpity, blump!* over and over, until they wound up, laughing, at the bottom.

"Last one up is a baby!" cried Raggedy Ann, as she scrambled to her feet. And with her skirts in her rag hands she went racing up the stairs to where the rest of the dollies stood laughing.

"Hurrah, for Raggedy Ann!" cried Raggedy Andy generously. "She won!"

The Beavers' Christmas Tree

An extract from *Pilgrims of the Wild*
by Grey Owl

*Grey Owl is a naturalist, and Anahareo is his native
American wife. They are living in a log cabin and have
adopted two beavers, McGinnis and McGinty, as pets.*

I arrived home in the thick of the blizzard
and found the little cabin mighty snug to
come into out of the storm. Anahareo had
busied herself crocheting bright wool
borders on white sugar bags, split open and
freshly laundered, and we now had these

for window curtains, which gave everything a cosy, homey appearance.

Anahareo said the beavers had missed me. McGinnis especially had seemed to search for something, and had spent much time at the door, looking up at it. I offered them the sticks of candy I had for them, and which they sat and ate with loud and most unmannerly sounds of satisfaction.

I laid out my small purchases, which the kindly storekeeper had suggested that I make, saying as he did so, that it must be lonesome in the woods and that he liked to feel that we had Christmas back there too. And being now in a country where Christmas was recognized as a real festival, we decided that we ought to make all the good cheer we could and so forget our troubles for a while.

Personally I had always been too busy hunting to celebrate the festive season. But I was now a family man, and being sure of the date, we would now keep it in style.

I whittled out some boards of dry cedar, painted them with Indian designs, and attached them to the sides and tops of the windows where they looked, if not too closely inspected, like plaques of beadwork. We painted hanging ornaments with tribal emblems and hung them in places where the light fell on them. We laid two rugs of deerskin, which were immediately seized as play-toys by the two beavers, and had to be nailed down. We distributed coloured candles in prominent places, and hung a Japanese lantern from the rafter.

On Christmas Eve all was ready. But there was one thing missing. Anahareo decided that the beavers were to have a Christmas tree. So while I lit the lantern and arranged the candles so their light fell on the decorations to the best advantage, and put apples and oranges and nuts in dishes on the table, and tended the saddle of deer meat that sizzled alongside of the factory-made Christmas pudding that was boiling on top of the little stove, Anahareo took an axe and snowshoes and went out into the starry Christmas night.

She was gone a little longer than I expected, and on looking out I saw her standing in rapt attention, listening. I asked her what she heard.

"Listen." She spoke softly. "Hear the Christmas bells," and pointed upwards.

I listened. A light breeze had sprung up and was flowing, humming in the pine tops far above. The breeze was whispering at first, then swelling louder in low undulating waves of sound, and sinking to a murmur, then ascending to a deep strong wavering note, fading again to a whisper. The pine trees – our Christmas bells.

Anahareo had got a fine balsam fir, a very picture of a Christmas tree, which she wedged upright in a crevice in the floor poles. On top of it she put a lit candle, and on the limbs tied candies, pieces of apple and small delicacies from the table, so they hung there by strings and could be reached.

The beavers viewed these preparations with no particular enthusiasm, but before long, attracted by the odour of the tree, they found the hanging titbits and sampled them. Soon they were busy cutting the strings and pulling them down, and eating

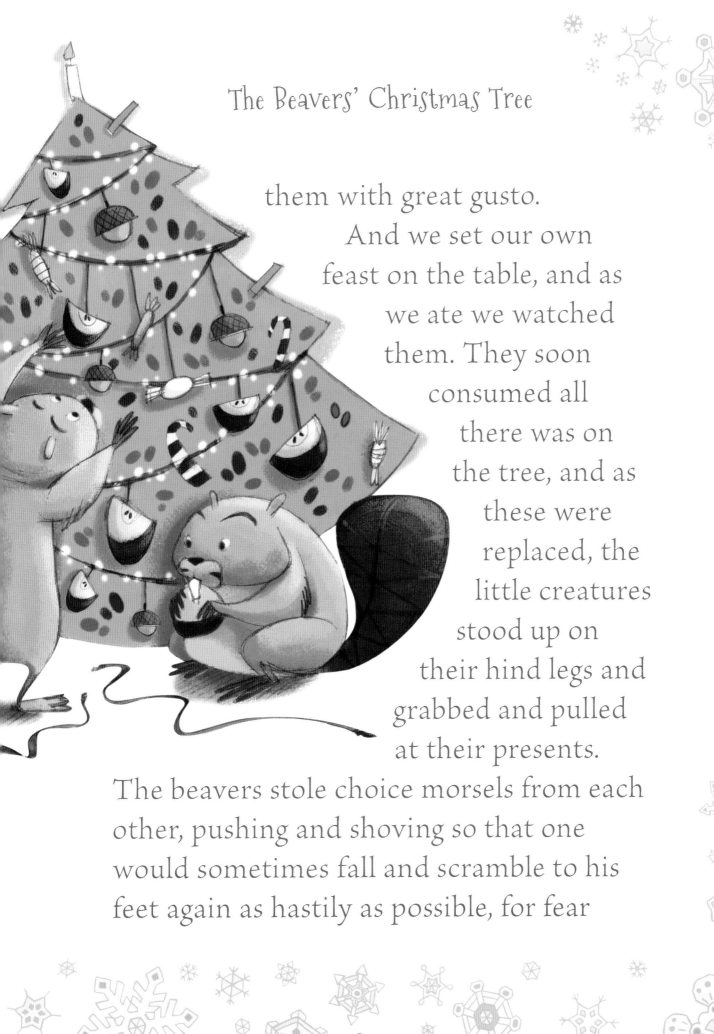

The Beavers' Christmas Tree

them with great gusto. And we set our own feast on the table, and as we ate we watched them. They soon consumed all there was on the tree, and as these were replaced, the little creatures stood up on their hind legs and grabbed and pulled at their presents.

The beavers stole choice morsels from each other, pushing and shoving so that one would sometimes fall and scramble to his feet again as hastily as possible, for fear everything would be gone before he got up, while they screeched and chattered and squealed in their excitement.

We forgot our supper, and laughed and called out to them, and they would run to us excitedly and back to the tree with little noises as if to say, 'Look what we found!'

And when they could eat no more they started to carry away titbits, sometimes between their teeth, on all fours, or staggering along upright with some prized titbit clutched tightly in their arms, each apparently bent on getting all that could be got while it lasted.

And when we thought they had enough and no longer made replacements, McGinty, the wise and the thrifty, pulled down the tree and started away with it, as though she figured on another crop

appearing later and had decided to corner the source of supply.

It was the best fun of the evening, and instead of us making a festival for them, they made one for us, and provided us with a Christmas entertainment such as had never before been seen in any other home, I'm pretty sure. And Anahareo was so happy to see her tree well appreciated, and the beavers were so happy to use it, and everybody seemed to be so thoroughly enjoying themselves, that I must be happy too just to see them so.

The Wild Wood in Winter

Adapted from *The Wind in the Willows*
by Kenneth Grahame

*Mole and Rat live together. Mole has often wanted
to meet Mr Badger, but Badger lives in the Wild Wood
and Rat has told Mole never to go there.*

There was plenty to talk about on those short winter days when the animals found themselves round the fire. Still, the Mole had a good deal of spare time on his hands, and so one afternoon he decided to go and explore the Wild Wood, and perhaps meet Mr Badger.

It was a cold, still afternoon when the Mole slipped out of the warm parlour into the open air, and pushed on towards the Wild Wood. There was nothing to alarm him at first entry. Twigs crackled under his feet, logs tripped him, but that was all fun and exciting.

Then the faces began.

It was over his shoulder, that he first thought he saw a face, a little, evil face, looking out at him from a hole. When he turned, the thing had vanished.

The Mole passed another hole, and another, and another. And then – yes! – no! – yes! Certainly a little, narrow face, with hard eyes, had flashed up for an instant, and was gone. If he could only get away from the holes in the banks, he thought, there

would be no more faces. He swung off the path and plunged into the untrodden places of the wood.

Then the whistling began.

Very faint and shrill it was, and far behind him, but somehow it made him hurry forwards. Then, still very faint and shrill, it sounded far ahead of him, and made him hesitate and want to go back. As the Mole stood still, a rabbit came running hard towards him. He waited, expecting it to swerve from him. Instead, the animal almost brushed him as it dashed past.

"Get out of this, you fool, get out!" the Mole heard him mutter as he disappeared down a friendly burrow.

In panic, the Mole began to run too. He ran up against things, he fell over things and into things. At last he took refuge in the

deep, dark hollow of an old beech tree. He was too tired to run, and could only snuggle down into the dry leaves and hope he was now safe for a time.

Meantime the Rat, warm and comfortable, dozed by his fireside. Then the fire crackled and he woke with a start. He reached down to the floor for his verses, and then looked round for the Mole.

But the Mole was not there.

The Rat left the house and carefully examined the ground outside, hoping to

find the Mole's tracks. There they were, sure enough, leading directly into the Wild Wood. The Rat re-entered the house, strapped a belt round his waist, shoved a brace of pistols into it and set off for the Wild Wood.

It was already getting towards dusk when he plunged into the wood, all the time calling out cheerfully, "Moly! Where are you? It's me – it's old Rat!"

He had patiently hunted through the wood for an hour or more, when at last he heard a little answering cry. He made his way to the foot of an old beech tree, with a hole in it, and from out of the hole came a voice, saying, "Ratty! Is that really you?"

The Rat crept into the hollow, and there, sure enough, he found the Mole, exhausted and still trembling.

"Oh Rat!" the Mole cried, "I've been so terribly frightened!"

"I quite understand," said the Rat soothingly. "You shouldn't really have gone and done it, Mole."

The Mole was greatly cheered by the sight of the Rat and he stopped shivering.

"Now then," said the Rat, "we really must make a start for home. It will never do to spend the night here. It is far too cold, for one thing."

"Dear Ratty," said the Mole, "I'm sorry, but you must let me rest here a while longer, if I'm to get home at all."

"Oh, all right," said the Rat, "rest away."

So the Mole got well into the dry leaves and presently dropped off into sleep, while the Rat covered himself up, too, and lay patiently waiting.

WINTER WONDERLAND

When at last the Mole woke up, the Rat said, "Now then! We really must be off."

He put his head out. Then the Mole heard him saying quietly to himself, "Hello."

"What's up, Ratty?" asked the Mole.

"Snow is up," replied the Rat briefly, "or rather, down. It's snowing hard. Still, we must make a start. The worst of it is, I don't exactly know where we are."

An hour or two later – they had lost all count of time – they pulled up. The snow was getting so deep that they could hardly drag their little legs through it. There seemed to be no end to this wood and, worst of all, no way out.

"We can't sit here very long," said the Rat. "There's a sort of dell down here where the ground seems all hilly and hummocky. We'll make our way into that, and try and

find some sort of shelter."

They were investigating one of the hummocky bits when the point of the Rat's stick struck something that sounded hollow. He worked till he could get a paw through, then called the Mole to come and help him. Hard at it went the two animals, till at last the result of their labours stood full in view.

In the side of what had seemed to be a snowbank stood a solid-looking little door. On a small brass plate, they could read by the aid of moonlight:

MR BADGER

The Mole fell backwards on the snow from sheer surprise and delight. "Rat!" he cried, "you're a wonder!" He sprang up at the bell pull, clutched it and swung there, and from quite a long way off they could faintly hear a deep-toned bell.

There was the noise of a bolt shot back, and the door opened a few inches, enough to show a long snout and a pair of sleepy blinking eyes.

"Now, the very next time this happens," said a gruff and suspicious voice, "I shall be exceedingly angry. Who is it this time, disturbing people on a night like this? Speak up now!"

"Oh, Badger," cried the Rat, "let us in, please. It's me, Rat, and my friend Mole, and we've lost our way in the snow."

"What, Ratty, my dear little man!"

exclaimed the Badger, in quite a different voice. "Come along in, both of you, at once. Well, I never! Lost in the snow!"

The two animals heard the door shut behind them with great joy and relief.

The Badger looked kindly down on them and patted both their heads. "This is not the sort of night for small animals to be out," he said. "Come into the kitchen. There's a first-rate fire there, and supper and everything."

He shuffled on in front of them, carrying the light, and they followed him, down a long, gloomy passage, into all the glow and warmth of a large fire-lit kitchen. The floor was well-worn red brick, and on the wide hearth burned a fire of logs.

The kindly Badger thrust them down on a settle to toast themselves at the fire, and he bade them remove their wet coats and boots. Then he fetched them both dressing-gowns and slippers.

In the embracing light and warmth, warm and dry at last, with weary legs propped up in front of them, and a clink of plates being arranged on the table behind, it seemed to the storm-driven animals that the cold

223

and trackless Wild Wood, just left outside, was miles and miles away, and all that they had suffered in it a half-forgotten dream.

Jingle Bells

By James Lord Pierpont

Dashing through the snow
In a one-horse open sleigh,
O'er the fields we go,
Laughing all the way.
Bells on bobtail ring,
Making spirits bright,
What fun it is to laugh and sing
A sleighing song tonight.

WINTER WONDERLAND

(Chorus)
Jingle bells, jingle bells,
Jingle all the way;
Oh, what fun it is to ride
In a one-horse open sleigh.
Jingle bells, jingle bells,
Jingle all the way;
Oh, what fun it is to ride
In a one-horse open sleigh.

A day or two ago,
I thought I'd take a ride
And soon Miss Fanny Bright
Was seated by my side,
The horse was lean and lank,
Misfortune seemed his lot,
He got into a drifted bank,
And then we got upsot.
Chorus: Jingle bells, jingle bells...

Jingle Bells

A day or two ago,
The story I must tell,
I went out on the snow,
And on my back I fell;
A gent was riding by
In a one-horse open sleigh,
He laughed as there I sprawling lie,
But quickly drove away.
Chorus: Jingle Bells, jingle bells...

Now the ground is white,
Go it while you're young,
Take the girls tonight,
And sing this sleighing song;
Just get a bobtailed bay,
Two forty as his speed,
Hitch him to an open sleigh
And crack! You'll take the lead.
Chorus: Jingle Bells, jingle bells...

PRESENTS AND PARTIES

Katy and Clover's Christmas

An extract from *What Katy Did at School*
by Susan Coolidge

*It is Christmas Eve, and Katy, Clover and their friend
Rose Red are at a boarding school, run by the strict Mrs Nipson.
The girls stay at school for Christmas, and though they are all
hoping their parents will have sent them boxes full of
Christmas presents, nothing has arrived.*

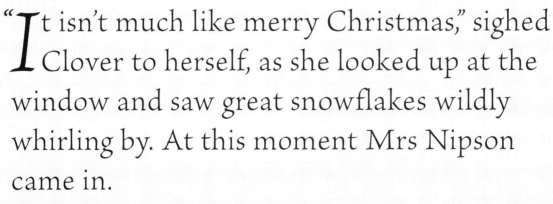

"*I*t isn't much like merry Christmas," sighed Clover to herself, as she looked up at the window and saw great snowflakes wildly whirling by. At this moment Mrs Nipson came in.

"Miss Carr, come here for a moment, if you please."

Clover, wondering, followed her.

"A parcel has arrived for you, and a box," said Mrs Nipson. "I will have the nails removed, and both of them placed in your room, but I expect you to refrain from examining them until tomorrow."

"Very well, ma'am," said Clover.

Study hour seemed unusually long that night. The minute it was over, the sisters ran to No. 2. There stood the boxes, a big wooden one and a small paper one. It was almost more than the girls could do to obey orders and not peep.

"I feel something hard," announced Clover, inserting a finger under the lid.

"Oh, do you?" cried Katy. Then, making a heroic effort, she jumped into the bed.

"It's the only way," she said. "Let's get to sleep as fast as we can, so as to make morning come quicker."

Katy dreamed of home that night. Perhaps it was that which made her wake so early. It was not five o'clock, and the room was dark. She lay perfectly still, for hours as it seemed. Then she could wait no longer, but crept out of bed and, raising the lid, put in her hand. Something crumby and sugary met it, and there, fitting

232

on her finger like a ring, was a round cake with a hole.

"Oh! It's one of Debby's jumbles!"

"Where? What? Give me one too!" cried Clover. The two lay nibbling the jumbles and talking about home till morning.

Breakfast was half an hour later than usual, which was comfortable. As soon as it was over, the girls proceeded to unpack their box. The day was so cold that they wrapped themselves in shawls, and Clover put on a hood and thick gloves. Rose Red, passing the door, recommended that she should add an umbrella.

"Come in," cried the sisters, "and help us open our box."

"Oh, by the way, you have a box, haven't you?" said Rose, who was perfectly aware of the important fact, and had presented

herself with the hope of being asked to look on. "Thank you, but perhaps I shall be in your way."

"You humbug!" said Clover. "You know you came on purpose!"

"Did I? Well, perhaps I did," laughed Rose. Then Katy lifted off the lid.

"Just look here!" she said.

The top of the box was mostly taken up with four square paper boxes, round which parcels of all shapes and sizes were wedged. One was of jumbles, another of ginger snaps, a third of crullers, and the fourth contained a big loaf of frosted plum cake.

"I never imagined anything so nice," declared Rose, with her mouth full of jumble. "As for those snaps, they're simply perfect. What can be in all those fascinating bundles? Do hurry and open one, Katy."

234

Katy and Clover's Christmas

Dear little Elsie! The first two bundles opened were hers, a white hood for Katy and a blue one for Clover, both of her own knitting. The girls were enchanted. They tried them on and spent so much time in admiring them that Rose grew impatient.

"I declare," she cried, "it isn't any of my funeral, I know, but if you don't open another parcel soon, I shall certainly fall to myself."

"Very well," said Katy, laying aside her hood, with one final glance. "Take out a bundle, Clover. It's your turn."

What fun it was opening those bundles! The girls made a long business of it, taking out but one at a time, exclaiming, admiring and exhibiting to Rose, before they began upon another. They laughed, they joked, but I do not think it would have taken

much to make either of them cry. Each separate article seemed full of the very look and feel of home.

"What can this be?" said Katy, as she unrolled a paper and disclosed a pretty round box. She opened it and gave a cry.

"Oh Clovy! Such a lovely thing! It's from Papa, of course it's from Papa."

The 'lovely thing' was a long slender chain for Katy's watch, worked in fine yellow gold. Clover's joy knew no bounds when further search revealed another box with a precisely similar chain for herself. "There never was such a papa in the world!" they said.

"Yes, there is. Mine is just as good," declared Rose. "I never saw such pretty chains in my life – never. Katy, I'm dying to know what is in the blue parcel."

The blue parcel contained a pretty blue ribbon for Clover. There was a pink one also, with a pink ribbon for Katy.

Everybody had thought of the girls. Old Mary sent them each a yard measure, and Miss Finch, a thread-case, stocked with differently coloured cottons. Alexander had

cracked a bag full of hickory nuts.

Never was such a wonderful box. It appeared to have no bottom whatever. Under the presents were parcels of figs, prunes, almonds, raisins, candy, and under those, apples and pears. There seemed no end to the surprises.

At last all were out.

"Now," said Katy, "I want you to help divide the other things, and make some packages for the girls. They are all disappointed not to have their boxes. I should like to have them share ours. Wouldn't you, Clover?"

"Yes. I was just going to propose it."

So Clover, Rose and Katy sorted ginger snaps and almonds and sugar plums and soon a gladsome crunching showed that the girls had found pleasant employment. None

of the snowed-up boxes got through till Monday, so except for Katy and Clover the school would have had no Christmas treat at all.

'The Carrs' Box' was always quoted as an example of what papas and mammas could accomplish, when they were of the right sort, and wanted to make schoolgirls happy.

Distributing their treasures kept Katy and Clover so busy that it was not until after dinner that they found time to open the smaller box. When they did so, they were sorry for the delay. The box was full of flowers – roses, red geranium leaves and white carnations.

Cousin Helen had sent them. And underneath, sewed to the box, that they might not shake about and do mischief, were two flat parcels wrapped in tissue

paper. They were glove cases, of quilted silk, delicately scented, one white, and one lilac, and to each was pinned a note, wishing the girls a Merry Christmas.

"How awfully good people are!" said Clover. "I do think we ought to be the best girls in the world."

The Christmas Party

By Frances Elizabeth Barrow

Mr and Mrs Percy had seven grandchildren – Mary, Carry, Thomas, Willy, Bella, Fanny, and finally Sarah. She was the youngest of the children, and they all loved her very much.

The children and their parents had been invited to eat Christmas dinner with their grandma. They were glad, for they liked to go to their grandma's very much.

At last Christmas Day came. It was a

bright, frosty day. The icicles that hung from the iron railing sparkled as the sun shone upon them, and everybody looked very happy indeed.

The children all got to their grandma's very nearly at the same time. The first thing they did was to run up to their grandma, and wish her a Merry Christmas and kiss her. Then they did the same to their grandpa. Then they all hugged and kissed each other, and jumped about so much, that some kissed noses and some kissed chins, and little Sarah was almost crazy with delight.

Soon the bell rang for dinner. It was now quite dark, and the chandelier that hung over the table was lit. The tablecloth was so white and fine that it looked like satin.

Would you like to know what they had

for dinner? Well, I will tell you. First they had some very nice soup. The children did not care for soup. Then they had some roast beef and a turkey. The children all took turkey.

Then came something that was quite astonishing. What do you think it was? It was a great plum pudding all on fire! It blazed away terribly, and Willy thought they had better send for the fire engines to put it out. But it was blown out easily, and the children each had a very small piece.

Very soon they got up and went upstairs

to the parlour. But what was that in the middle of the room? It seemed to be a large table covered all over with a cloth. What could it be?

Willy said, "Grandma, that table looks as if something was on it."

And little Sarah said, "Grandma, I guess Santa Claus has been here."

"Yes, dear children," said their grandma, "Santa Claus has been here, and this time he looked very much like your grandpa. He will be up soon, and then we will see what is on the table."

Oh how the children did wish to peep! They could not look at anything else. They danced and jumped round the table, and were in a great hurry for their grandpa. In a few minutes he came into the room, and went to the table and took the cloth off.

The Christmas Party

The table was covered with beautiful things, and under it was something that looked like a little red-brick house.

"Well," said their kind grandpa, "my dear children, you may go up to the table and see if you can find out who they are for."

The children gathered round the table, and Willy took from the top a fine boat with all her sails set. His eyes sparkled when he saw written on a slip of paper, which lay on the deck, these words, 'For my dear Willy'.

The children clapped their hands, and nothing was heard but, "How beautiful!"

"It is a ship of war," said Willy, "only look at the little brass guns on her deck! Thank you, dear Grandpa. What is the name of my ship?"

"Her name is painted on her stern," said his grandpa. Willy looked and saw that she was called the 'Louisa'. The other children laughed, for Willy knew a very pretty little girl whose name was Louisa, and he liked her very much.

After they had all admired the boat, they

went back to the table, and there were two beautiful picture books, one for Bella and one for Mary. Next to these was a large doll for Carry and another for Fanny.

Carry's doll was dressed in blue satin, with a white satin hat, and Fanny's doll was dressed in pink satin, with a black velvet hat and feathers.

They hugged their dolls to their little breasts, and then ran to hug and kiss their grandpa. Carry said, "My dolly's name shall be Rose," and Fanny said, "My dolly's name shall be Christmas, because I got her on Christmas Day."

Well I must hurry and tell you the rest, for I am afraid my story is getting too long. Thomas found for him a splendid zoo, and all the animals made noises like real animals. There were roaring lions, and

yelling tigers, and laughing hyenas, and chattering monkeys, and growling bears, and many other wild beasts. Oh how pleased Thomas was, and all the children!

Little Sarah did nothing but jump up and down and say, "So many things! I never saw so many things!"

But who was to have the little house under the table, I wonder? There was a little piece of paper sticking out of the chimney, and Sarah pulled it out and carried it to her grandpa. He took her up in his arms and read it to her. It said, "A little house for my little darling Sarah."

"It is for me," said the little girl. "My name is Sarah, and it must be for me."

Her grandpa drew the little house out and opened it. The whole front of the house opened, and there were two rooms –

one was a parlour and one a bedroom. The children all cried out, "Look at the table, and the red velvet chairs, and the elegant curtains! Oh, how beautiful it is!"

Little Sarah did not say a word. She jumped up and down, her eyes shining like diamonds. She was too much pleased to speak. At last she said, "There is a young

lady sitting in the chair with a red sash on. I think she wants to come out."

"You may take her out," said her grandpa.

So Sarah took the young lady out, and then took up the chairs and sofa, one by one, and smoothed the velvet, and looked at the little clock on the mantelpiece, and opened the little drawers of the bureau, and then, she began to jump again.

There was never such a happy party before. The children hardly wished to dance, they were so busy looking at their presents. But after a little while they had a very nice dance.

It was now quite late, and little Sarah had fallen fast asleep on the sofa, with the young lady out of the little house clasped tight. So they wrapped her up, doll and all, in a great shawl, and the rest put on their

nice warm coats, and after a great deal of hugging and kissing, they went home happy and delighted.

So ended this joyful Christmas Day.

Kate and Dick's Christmas

By Fannie E Ostrander

Bessie and Clara were staying at their grandparents' house in the country for the summer, with their cousins Kate and Dick, where they enjoyed sharing a good many pets.

There were the sheepdogs Frisk and Ponto and Fuss, and another little dog called Fly. There was the pony, Fleet, and the newest pet of all was a dear little colt that Kate's papa had given to her for her

very own, because the pony she rode really belonged to Dick. This colt she had named Fairy, and she took great care of it.

Then the baby that they all loved lived here. Her name was May, and she was Kate and Dick's sister. She was a sweet little thing, just beginning to walk and to talk. She could say 'chicky' quite plainly, and she liked to toddle out and watch the little girls feed the chickens.

But I can't begin to tell you all the good times the children had that summer. They were happy all the time, and Grandma said they were so good that it was really no trouble at all to have them there.

But at last one Saturday evening, Papa, who always came out from the city to spend Sunday with them, said they must start for home the next Monday.

PRESENTS AND PARTIES

They did want to stay longer, but Papa laughed and said, "Christmas is coming now, you know, and Santa Claus couldn't bring things way out here as easy as he could get them to you in town."

Then the children began to think of Christmas, and to tease Grandpa and Grandma to come and spend it with them, and of course Papa and Mamma teased too, so at last they promised.

The children said goodbye to their pets, and to Kate and May and Dick, and went away shouting, "Goodbye, Grandma. Now remember you promised!"

After the children reached home they talked of Grandma's nearly all the time when they were not talking of Christmas. Bessie wrote a postcard to Santa Claus asking him to be sure to bring a pair of his

nicest gold-bowed spectacles for Grandma, because she had lost her old ones, and a gold-headed cane for Grandpa.

At last Christmas Eve came, and Grandma and Grandpa were there, and the children hung up their stockings, and Bessie said that Grandma and Grandpa

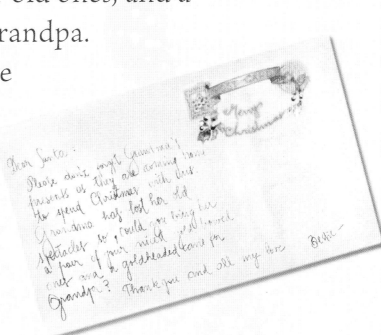

must be sure to hang up theirs too. Then, after they had gone to bed, the smaller children whispered for a long time about Santa Claus and listened to hear his sleigh bells on the roof.

"I don't see how he can get down the chimney," whispered Bessie. "You know he's so fat in all his pictures."

"Maybe he takes off his coat," whispered Clara, "then he wouldn't be quite so big." But she didn't see how he could get down the chimney, either.

Once or twice they were sure they heard him on the roof, and they covered up their heads so he wouldn't think they were peeping, and at last they went to sleep before they knew it.

Willie and Tom were just as anxious as the little girls, and whispered just as much.

Bessie and Clara were the first ones up. They shouted with delight when they looked in their stockings. There was a little doll in each stocking – a doll with real hair and eyes that opened and shut, and the dolls were dressed very prettily.

Willie found the funniest jumping-jack in his stocking, and Tom pulled a flute out

256

of his. He had everybody awake in no time after that!

Grace was happy when she looked in her stocking. There was a little box in it, and in the box was a lovely gold watch. Harry found just what he wanted too – a pair of skates.

But Grandma and Grandpa were surprised when they discovered the spectacles and the cane.

"Who could have told Santa what we wanted?" said Grandma.

PRESENTS AND PARTIES

Grandpa said he couldn't understand it either, and then Bessie had to tell the secret. She ran up to each of them and whispered, "I wrote to him myself!"

Then how they kissed her.

All day long the library was kept closed – not a child was allowed to peep in. But what fun they had all day, and what a Christmas dinner, with a plum pudding as big as a pumpkin.

In the evening the library door was opened, and there was the prettiest Christmas tree, all blazing with candles and hung with pretty things, while piled around it were books and toys and everything that everybody wanted most.

And there, lying in front of the tree and looking as happy as the children themselves, was a great, big, noble dog, who got up and

came to meet them as they trooped in.

"Oo! Oo! Oo!" cried Bessie, bending to pat the big dog's head. "What's your name, you great, big darling? Oo! Oo! Whose is he, Papa?"

"Ask Santa Claus," said Papa, and sure enough, Santa Claus stepped out from behind the tree.

"His name is on his collar," Santa Claus said to Bessie.

Then the children all rushed for him, for they knew it was Grandpa dressed up like Santa Claus.

Afterwards Bessie spelled out the dog's name, 'C-a-r-l-o', on his collar, and her own on a card which was tied to it, and she was the happiest little girl in the world.

But everyone else was happy too. They all said it was the very merriest Christmas

they had ever seen, and Clara and Bessie dreamed that Santa Claus told them he himself had never had so much fun before.

Thank You Letters

An extract from *Betty Trevor*
by Mrs G De Horne Vaizey

*Betty and Jill (whose full name is Margaret) are
sisters. A sovereign was a gold coin, and a crown was a
silver one, both worth quite a generous amount of
money when this story was written.*

*B*etty Trevor shivered up in her attic
bedroom, putting in the last stitches
to the presents that she was making at the
cost of much trouble. Jill was invited to the
private view, her own present being hidden
away, and expressed admiration.

"Such a lot of work though!" she declared. "Look at me, I've done the whole thing in one afternoon! Sailed out with my savings in my purse – and I got fifteen really handsome presents."

"Jill, you haven't! It isn't possible!"

"It is. It only needs management. I've kept all the chocolate boxes we have had given to us during the year – six of them – and they look wonderful filled with sweets at sixpence a pound. I collected mother's old scent bottles too, and bought a shilling's worth of eau de Cologne to fill them. Such a joke! It didn't quite go round, so I put some water in the last, and it's turned quite milky. I'll have to give that to Pam. She'll think it something new and superior. I've got sticking-plaster for the boys – they are sure to cut their fingers some day – and a

beautiful needle book for Mother."

She skipped downstairs and, sitting down in the drawing room, proceeded to write a number of letters, in which words and spaces were curiously mingled.

Dear Aunt Margaret, thank you so much for the beautiful... It is just what I wanted. It was so nice of you to send it to me. I think it is... I hope you are quite well, and not having asthma any more... Your loving niece, Margaret.

Darling Cousin Flo, I am so awfully obliged to you for the lovely... It is just what I wanted.

Thank You Letters

I am so pleased to have it. It will just do for... I think Christmas is ripping, don't you? Please write soon.

Dear Mrs Gregory, it is most kind of you to remember me with such a nice present. The... is just what I wanted. I am much obliged to you for remembering me. Has not Christmas Day been... this year? I am your loving little friend, Margaret Meredith Trevor.

My own dear, darling Norah, what an angel you are to send me that perfectly lovely... It is just exactly what I wanted, and I am so proud to have it. Come round tomorrow and see my things. I've got... altogether. Isn't that a lot? Don't you call this weather...? Your own Jill.

She was scribbling away when a hand fell

on her shoulder and a voice cried, "Eh, what? Too busy to hear me come in, were you? What's the meaning of this?"

Starting up, she saw General Digby bending over her. This was not the first visit which the General had paid. He was a lonely old man, and to spend a few minutes in the cheery atmosphere of a family made a pleasant break for him.

"Writing Christmas letters, eh?" boomed the General loudly. "Sending off your presents, I suppose. What? Thanking people for presents, do you say? That's a bit previous, isn't it? What's the hurry?"

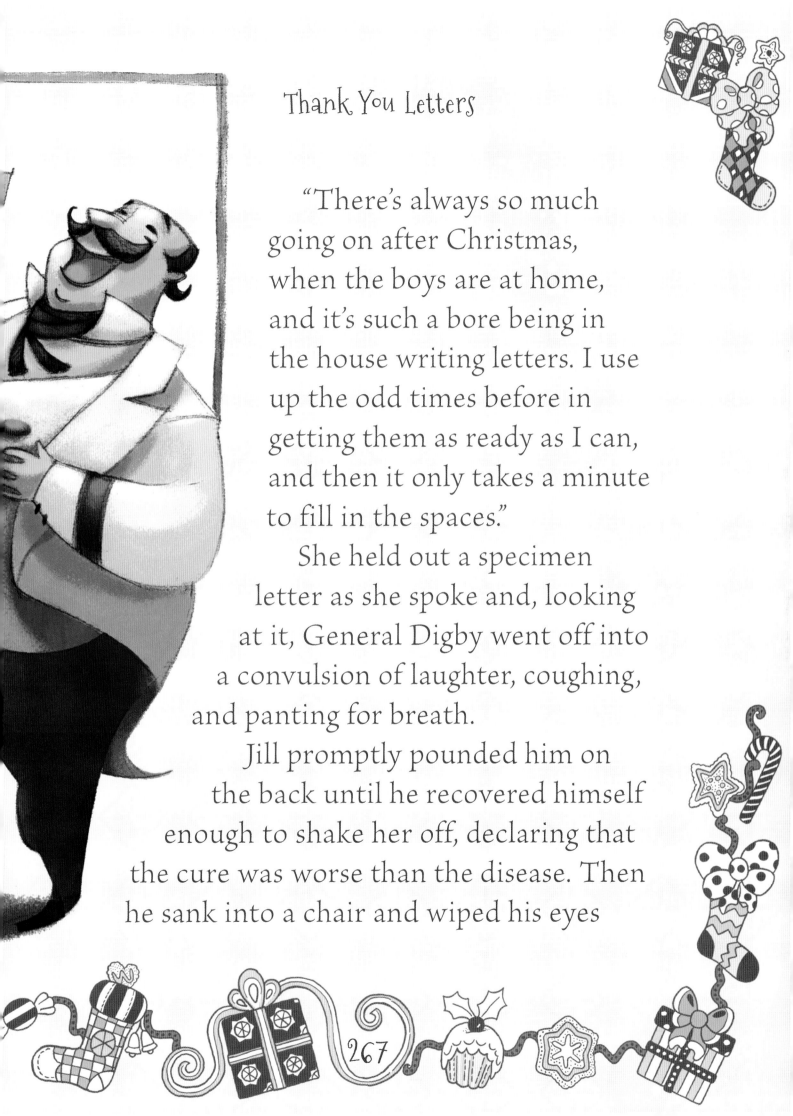

Thank You Letters

"There's always so much going on after Christmas, when the boys are at home, and it's such a bore being in the house writing letters. I use up the odd times before in getting them as ready as I can, and then it only takes a minute to fill in the spaces."

She held out a specimen letter as she spoke and, looking at it, General Digby went off into a convulsion of laughter, coughing, and panting for breath.

Jill promptly pounded him on the back until he recovered himself enough to shake her off, declaring that the cure was worse than the disease. Then he sank into a chair and wiped his eyes

with a handkerchief.

"Where's my letter?" he inquired. "I suppose there's one addressed to me among all that number. Was I as fortunate as the rest in sending just what was wanted? You are a young woman of a great many wants, it seems to me. Tell you what now – I'll strike a bargain! Fill up the blanks, and I'll see if I can come up to expectation!"

"Oh no!" cried Jill, blushing with embarrassment. "There is no letter for you. I truly never thought you would give us anything. I couldn't possibly choose myself. It's awfully good of you to think of it, but, really, anything. It's like this, you see – I want anything I can get!"

"Oh, you do, do you?" cried the General. "Nothing like honesty in this world, my dear. Well, we must see what we can do! I'll

bend my mind to the question, and you shall know the result on Christmas Day."

The Trevors' programme on Christmas Day differed from those of their friends. No presents were given in the morning. It was enough excitement to know that it was Christmas Day, and to linger over a late and luxurious breakfast before going to church. On their return, the first sight of the hall table banished every other thought, for on it lay a pile of Christmas cards.

Betty pounced on them, and gave a shout of delight.

"There's money inside! There is, I can feel it. Mine's quite small – like a – a—"

She opened her own in a flutter of excitement. Inside there was a folded piece of paper enclosing a second envelope. In her haste Betty ripped it open, and held up to

view a brand new sovereign.

"It is! It is! How simply lovely! I was so hard up – and now! What angel can have sent it?"

She picked up the piece of paper which she had dropped in her haste, and read aloud, "With the best wishes of General Digby."

Jack and Jill had each a new ten-shilling piece, and Pam a magnificent silver crown.

"He said he would send me something, but I never thought it would be money. It's what I like better than anything else, to be rich in the Christmas holidays!" Jill cried.

Mrs Trevor smiled and said, "So he seemed to think. He asked my permission before sending his presents in this form, and said he would like to give you money,

because when he was a boy an old lady used to send new coins to himself and his brothers every Christmas, and he had never forgotten the pleasure they gave him."

Christmas Morning

An extract from *Peter and Polly in Winter*
by Rose Lucia

Early Christmas morning Peter awoke. He heard a noise in Mother's room, so he knew that he might get up.

He pushed open the door. "Merry Christmas! Merry Christmas!" he shouted.

"Merry Christmas," said Mother, hugging him tightly.

"Merry Christmas," said Father, tossing him up into the air. "Did you see Santa Claus last night?"

Christmas Morning

Just then Polly ran in. "Oh, oh, it is Christmas!" she cried. "Merry Christmas! Merry Christmas! Just see what I found in my bed."

It was a box of animal crackers. They were all sheep.

"Oh Father! You did it for a joke. You know I do not like mutton."

There were to be no more presents until after breakfast, so the children dressed quickly. It was very hard for them to eat anything at all.

At last Polly said, "I cannot wait another second. I will eat my breakfast with my dinner. Here comes Grandmother. Now may we open the door and see the tree?"

"In just a minute," said Father. "You say 'Merry Christmas' to Grandmother. I have one last thing for the tree. You may come in

when I call." And out he ran.

"I wonder what it is," said Polly, excitedly. "I can hear him coming back through the side door."

Then Grandmother came in, and Polly forgot to wonder any more.

At last they heard Father shout, "Come!"

Polly opened the door, and the children rushed in.

"Oh! Oh!" said Polly.

"Oh! Oh!" said Peter.

Such a beautiful tree they had never before seen. It was hung with strings of popped corn and red cranberries. It was covered with coloured balls and big gold stars. Over it was white, shiny stuff that looked like snow.

It had candy bags and oranges. At the top, there was a doll with wings. And there

were many boxes and packages.

"Oh! Oh! Oh!" said both children again.

"Do you like it?" asked Mother.

"I never saw anything so pretty," said Polly. "Is that a fairy at the top?"

"I think it is Santa Claus' little girl," said Peter. "I should very much like to have her for my own."

"Should you rather have that than anything else here?" asked Father.

"I think so, Father. May I?"

"Walk around the tree and see if you are sure, my son."

Peter did as he was told. He had not taken many steps when he jumped back with a cry.

"What is it? What is it?" he asked.

Polly ran forwards, and what do you think she saw?

On the other side of the tree
something moved. Polly saw
two large eyes, two long ears,
a brown head, and then she
knew that it was a pony.

"Peter, Peter!" she
cried, "here is the

pony! It is on the Christmas tree! O Peter, Peter, Peter!"

"Lead her out," said Father. "She will come with you. She likes children."

So Polly took hold of the pony's little strap, and the pony walked out into the room after her.

"Her name is Brownie," said Father. "She is Grandmother's present to you and Peter. She is half yours and half Peter's."

"Oh, Grandmother!" cried Polly. "I thank you now, but I will thank you even better before long."

"Which half is mine, Grandmother?" asked Peter.

"Half of both halves," Grandmother replied. "Why?"

"Nothing," said Peter. "I love both her halves. And I love you, too. And I love the

tree, and Christmas, and everybody."

"And so you should," said Father. "Come now, we will take Brownie to her stable. Then you may get the presents off the tree."

The Josephs' Christmas

By L M Montgomery

*T*he month before Christmas was always the most exciting and mysterious time in the Joseph household. Such scheming and planning, such counting of small hoards, such hiding and smuggling of things out of sight, as went on among the little Josephs!

During this particular December the planning and contriving had been more difficult and the results less satisfactory

than usual. The Josephs were poor at any time, but this winter they were poorer than ever. But on Christmas Eve every little Joseph went to bed with a clear conscience, for was there not on the corner table in the kitchen a small mountain of tiny – sometimes very tiny – gifts labelled with the names of recipients and givers?

It was beginning to snow when the small, small Josephs went to bed, and when the big, small Josephs climbed the stairs it was snowing thickly.

Mr and Mrs Joseph sat down before the fire and listened to the wind howling about the house.

"I'm glad I'm not driving over the prairie

tonight," said Mr Joseph. "It's quite a storm. Mary, this is the first Christmas since we came west that we couldn't afford some little extras for them, even if it was only a box of nuts and candy."

Mrs Joseph sighed over Jimmy's worn jacket that she was mending, but then she smiled at Mr Joseph.

"Never mind, John," she said. "Things will be better next Christmas, we'll hope. We've got each other, and good health and spirits, and a Christmas wouldn't be much without those if we had all the presents in the world."

Mr Joseph nodded.

"That's so. I don't want to grumble, but I did want to get Maggie a 'real live doll', as she calls it. There was one at Fisher's store today – a big beauty with real hair, and eyes

281

that opened and shut. Just fancy Maggie's face if she saw that tomorrow morning."

"Don't let's fancy it," laughed Mrs Joseph, "That can't be someone at the door!"

"It is, though," said Mr Joseph as he strode to the door and flung it open.

Two snowed-up figures were standing on the porch. As they stepped in, the Josephs recognized one of them as Mr Ralston, a wealthy merchant in a small town fifteen miles away.

"Late hour for callers, isn't it?" said Mr Ralston. "The fact is, our horse has about given out, and the storm is so bad that we can't proceed. This is my wife, and we are on our way to spend Christmas with my brother's family at Lindsay. Can you take us in for the night, Mr Joseph?"

"Certainly, and welcome!" exclaimed

Mr Joseph heartily. "I'll see to putting your horse away now, Mr Ralston. This way, if you please."

When the two men came into the house again, Mrs Ralston and Mrs Joseph were sitting at the fire. Mr Ralston put the big basket he was carrying down on a bench in the corner.

"Thought I'd better bring our Christmas flummery in," he said. "You see, Mrs Joseph, my brother has a big family, so we are taking them a lot of Santa Claus stuff. Mrs Ralston packed this basket, and goodness knows what she put in it, but she half cleaned out my store."

Mrs Joseph gave a little sigh in spite of herself, and looked wistfully at the heap of gifts on the corner table.

Mrs Ralston looked too.

"Santa Claus seems to have visited you already," she said.

The Josephs laughed.

"Our Santa Claus is somewhat out of pocket this year," said Mr Joseph frankly.

A shakedown was spread in the kitchen for the unexpected guests, and presently the Ralstons found themselves alone. Mrs Ralston went over to the Christmas table and looked at the little gifts half tenderly and half pityingly.

"They're not much like the contents of our basket, are they?" she said, as she touched the calendar Jimmie had made for Mollie out of cardboard and autumn leaves and grasses.

"Just what I was thinking," returned her husband, "and I was thinking of something else, too. I've a notion that I'd like to see

some of the things in our basket right here on this table."

"I'd like to see them all on this table," said Mrs Ralston promptly. "Let's just leave them here, Edward. Roger's family will have plenty of presents without them, and for that matter we can send them ours when we go back home."

"Just as you say," agreed Mr Ralston. "I very much like the idea of giving the small folk of this household a rousing good Christmas for once."

Then by comparing the names attached to the gifts on the table they managed to divide theirs up pretty evenly among the little Josephs.

When all was done Mrs Ralston said, "We will be going before daylight, probably, and in the hurry of getting off I hope that

PRESENTS AND PARTIES

Mr and Mrs Joseph will not notice the difference till we're gone."

It fell out as Mrs Ralston had planned. Breakfast for the travellers was cooked and eaten by lamplight, then the horse and sleigh were brought to the door and Mr Ralston carried out his empty basket.

"Goodbye and a merry Christmas to you all," he said.

Mrs Joseph went back to the kitchen and her eyes fell on the heaped-up table in the corner.

"Why—!" Mrs Joseph said, and snatched off the cover.

Mr Joseph came too, and looked and whistled in shock.

There really seemed to be everything on that table that the hearts of children could desire – three pairs of skates, a fur cap, half a dozen gleaming new books, a writing desk, a pair of fur-topped gloves, and a china cup and saucer.

All these were to be seen at the first glance, and in one corner of the table was a big box filled with candies and nuts and raisins, and in the other, a doll with curling golden hair and brown eyes, dressed in real clothes and with all her wardrobe in a trunk beside her. Pinned to her dress was a note with Maggie's name written on it.

"The children will go wild with delight,"

said Mrs Joseph happily.

They pretty nearly did when they all came scrambling down the stairs a little later.

Such a Christmas had never been known in the Joseph household before. Maggie clasped her doll with shining eyes. And as for the big box of good things, why, everybody appreciated that.

I'm glad to be able to say, too, that the little Josephs did not forget to appreciate the gifts they had prepared for each other. Mollie thought her calendar just too pretty

for anything, and Jimmie was sure the new mittens that Maggie had knitted for him were the nicest mittens ever worn.

The Cratchits' Christmas Goose

An extract from *A Christmas Carol*
by Charles Dickens

*The Cratchit family are a poor family living in Victorian London.
Martha works away from home, and only gets one day off. The
Cratchits have no oven, so their goose is cooked at the bakers and
then brought home, and they boil their pudding in the large
copper bowl, which they usually use for washing their clothes.*

"What has ever got your precious father then." said Mrs Cratchit. "And your brother, Tiny Tim! And Martha! She wasn't as late last Christmas Day by half an hour!"

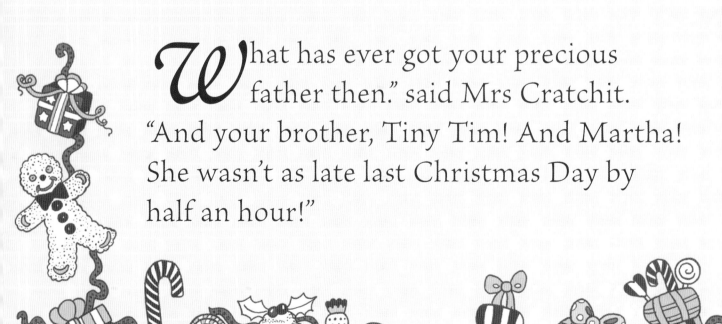

The Cratchits' Christmas Goose

"Here's Martha, Mother!" said a girl, appearing as she spoke.

"Here's Martha, Mother!" cried the two young Cratchits. "Hurrah! There's such a goose, Martha!"

"Why, bless your heart alive, my dear, how late you are!" said Mrs Cratchit, kissing her a dozen times, and taking off her shawl and bonnet for her.

"We'd a deal of work to finish up last night," replied the girl, "and had to clear away this morning, Mother!"

"Well! Never mind so long as you are come," said Mrs Cratchit. "Sit ye down before the fire, my dear, and have a warm, Lord bless ye!"

"No, no! There's Father coming," cried the two young Cratchits, who were everywhere at once. "Hide, Martha, hide!"

So Martha hid herself, and in came little Bob, the father, with at least three feet of comforter hanging down before him, and his threadbare clothes darned up and brushed to look seasonable, and Tiny Tim upon his shoulder. Alas for Tiny Tim, he bore a little crutch, and had his limbs supported by an iron frame.

"Why, where's our Martha?" cried Bob Cratchit, looking round.

"Not coming," said Mrs Cratchit.

"Not coming!" said Bob. "Not coming upon Christmas Day!"

Martha didn't like to see him disappointed, even if it were only in joke, so she came out from behind the closet door, and ran into his arms. The two young Cratchits hustled Tiny Tim, and bore him off into the wash house, that he might hear

the pudding singing in the copper.

"And how did little Tim behave?" asked Mrs Cratchit, when she had rallied Bob on his credulity and Bob had hugged his daughter to his heart's content.

"As good as gold," said Bob, "and better."

His little crutch was heard on the floor, and back came Tiny Tim before another word was spoken, escorted by his brother and sister to his stool before the fire.

And while Bob, turning up his cuffs, compounded some hot mixture in a jug with lemons, and stirred it round and round, and put it on the hob to simmer, Master Peter and the two young Cratchits went to fetch the goose, with which they soon returned in high procession.

You might have thought a goose the rarest of all birds, and in truth, it was

something like it in that house.

Mrs Cratchit made the gravy (ready beforehand in a little saucepan) hissing hot, Master Peter

mashed the potatoes with incredible vigour, Miss Belinda sweetened up the apple sauce, and Martha dusted the hot plates.

Bob took Tiny Tim beside him in a tiny corner, at the table. The two young Cratchits set chairs for everybody, not forgetting themselves, and mounting guard upon their posts, crammed spoons into their mouths, lest they should shriek for goose before their turn came to be helped.

At last the dishes were set on the table and grace was said. It was succeeded by a breathless pause, as Mrs Cratchit, looking slowly all along the carving knife, prepared to plunge it in the breast. But when she did, and when the long-expected gush of stuffing issued forth, one murmur of delight arose all around the table, and even Tiny Tim, excited by the two young Cratchits,

beat on the table with the handle of his knife, and cried hurrah!

There never was such a goose. Bob said he didn't believe there ever was such a goose cooked. Its tenderness and flavour, size and cheapness, were the themes of universal admiration.

Eked out by the apple sauce and mashed potatoes, it was a sufficient dinner for the whole family. Indeed, as Mrs Cratchit said with great delight (surveying one small atom of a bone on the dish), they hadn't eaten it all at last! Yet everyone had had enough, and the youngest Cratchits in particular were steeped in sage and onion to the eyebrows!

But now, the plates being changed by Miss Belinda, Mrs Cratchit left the room alone – too nervous to bear witnesses – to

take the pudding up and bring it in.

Suppose it should not be done enough? Suppose it should break in turning out? Suppose somebody should have got over the wall of the backyard and stolen the pudding, while they were merry with the goose? All sorts of horrors were supposed.

Hallo! A great deal of steam! The pudding was out of the copper. A smell like a washing day! That was the cloth. A smell like an eating house and a pastry cook's next door to each other, with a laundress next door to that! That was the pudding.

In half a minute Mrs Cratchit entered, flushed, but smiling

proudly, carrying the pudding, which looked like a speckled cannonball, so hard and firm, blazing in half of half-a-quartern of ignited brandy, and with Christmas holly stuck into the top.

Oh, a wonderful pudding! Bob Cratchit said, and calmly too, that he regarded it as the greatest success Mrs Cratchit had achieved since their marriage. Mrs Cratchit said that now the weight was off her mind, she would confess she had had her doubts about the quantity of flour.

Everybody had something to say about it, but nobody said or thought it was at all a small pudding for so large a family. It would have been flat heresy to do so. And any Cratchit would have blushed to hint at such a thing.

At last the dinner was all done, the cloth

was cleared, the hearth swept, and the fire made up.

The compound in the jug being tasted and considered perfect, apples and oranges were put upon the table, and a shovelful of chestnuts on the fire.

Then all the Cratchit family drew round the hearth, in what Bob Cratchit called a circle, meaning half a one. And at Bob Cratchit's elbow stood the family display of glass – two tumblers, and a custard-cup without a handle.

These held the hot stuff from the jug, however, as well as golden goblets would have done, and Bob served it out with beaming looks, while the chestnuts on the fire sputtered and cracked noisily.

Then Bob proposed, "A Merry Christmas to us all, my dears. God bless us!"

Which all the family re-echoed.

"God bless us every one!" said Tiny Tim, the last of all.

Figgy Pudding

Traditional

We wish you a Merry Christmas
We wish you a Merry Christmas
We wish you a Merry Christmas
and a Happy New Year.
Good tidings we bring to you and your kin
We wish you a Merry Christmas and
a Happy New Year.

Figgy Pudding

Now bring us some figgy pudding
Now bring us some figgy pudding
Now bring us some figgy pudding
and bring some out here.

We wish you a Merry Christmas…

For we all like figgy pudding
For we all like figgy pudding
For we all like figgy pudding
so bring some out here.

We wish you a Merry Christmas…

And we won't go until we've got some
And we won't go until we've got some
And we won't go until we've got some
so bring some out here.

We wish you a Merry Christmas…

GOODWILL AND GIVING

The First Stockings

An extract from *The Life and Adventures of Santa Claus*
by L Frank Baum

*This is part of a story telling how Santa Claus invented
the first toys and then, with the help of his reindeers Flossie
and Glossie, took them to children's houses.*

When you remember that no child,
until Santa Claus began his travels,
had ever known the pleasure of possessing a
toy, you will understand how joy crept into
the homes of those who had been favoured
with a visit from the good man. They

talked of him day by day in loving tones and were grateful for his kindly deeds.

When another Christmas Eve drew near there was a monster load of beautiful gifts for the children ready to be loaded upon the big sledge. Claus filled three sacks to the brim, and tucked every corner of the sledge full of toys besides.

Then, at twilight, the ten reindeer appeared and Flossie introduced them all to Claus. They were Racer and Pacer, Reckless and Speckless, Fearless and Peerless, and Ready and Steady, who, with Glossie and Flossie, made up the ten who have traversed the world these hundreds of years with their generous master. They were all very beautiful, with slender limbs, spreading antlers, velvety dark eyes and smooth coats of fawn colour spotted with white.

GOODWILL AND GIVING

Claus loved them at once, and has loved them ever since, for they are loyal friends and have rendered him priceless service.

The new harness fitted them nicely and soon they were all fastened to the sledge by twos, with Glossie and Flossie in the lead. The reindeer wore strings of sleigh bells, and were so delighted with the music they made that they kept prancing up and down to make the bells ring.

Claus seated himself in the sledge, drew a warm robe over his knees and his fur cap over his ears, and

The First Stockings

cracked his whip as a signal to start.

Instantly the ten reindeer leapt forwards and were away just like the wind, while jolly Santa Claus laughed gleefully to see them run, and shouted a song in his big, hearty voice:

> *With a ho, ho, ho!*
> *And a ha, ha, ha!*
> *And a ho, ho, ha, ha, hee!*
> *Now away we go*
> *O'er the frozen snow,*
> *As merry as we can be!*
> *There are many joys*
> *In our load of toys,*
> *As many a child will know;*
> *We'll scatter them wide*
> *On our wild night ride*
> *O'er the crisp and sparkling snow!*

GOODWILL AND GIVING

Now it was on this Christmas Eve that little Margot and her brother Dick, and her cousins Ned and Sara, who were visiting at Margot's house, came in from making a snowman. The children's clothes were damp, their mittens dripping, and their shoes and stockings wet through and through. They were not scolded, for Margot's mother knew the snow was melting, but they were sent to bed early so that their clothes might be hung over chairs to dry.

The shoes were placed on the red tiles of the hearth, where the heat from the hot embers would strike them, and the stockings were carefully hung in a row by the chimney, directly over the fireplace.

That was the reason Santa Claus noticed them when he came down the chimney that night, and all the household were fast asleep. He was in a tremendous hurry, and seeing the stockings all belonged to children, he quickly stuffed his toys into them and dashed up the chimney again, appearing on the roof so suddenly that the reindeer were astonished at his agility.

'I wish they would all hang up their

stockings,' he thought, as he drove to the next chimney. 'It would save me a lot of time and I could then visit more children before daybreak.'

When Margot and Dick and Ned and Sara jumped out of bed the next morning and ran downstairs to get their stockings from the fireplace, they were filled with delight to find the toys from Santa Claus inside them. In fact, I think they found more presents in their stockings than any other children of that city had received, for Santa Claus was in a hurry and did not stop to count the toys.

The children told all their little friends about it, and of course every one of them decided to hang their own stockings by the fireplace the next Christmas Eve.

On his next trip Santa Claus found so

many stockings hung up in anticipation of his visit that he could fill them in a jiffy and be away again in half the time required to find the children and place the toys by their bedsides.

The custom grew year after year, and has always been a great help to Santa Claus. And, with so many children to visit, he surely needs all the help we can give him.

The Little Match Girl

Adapted from a story by
Hans Christian Andersen

*I*t was dreadfully cold. It was snowing fast and was almost dark as evening came on. In the cold and the darkness went a poor little girl, walking slowly along the street barefoot. When she left home she had shoes on, but they were much too big for her feet and the poor little girl lost them in running across the street. When she looked for them, one was not to be found, and a boy grabbed the other and ran away with it.

The Little Match Girl

So on the little girl went with her bare feet that were blue with cold. In an old apron that she wore were bundles of matches, which she sold to passersby to make a few pennies each day, and she carried a bundle also in her hand. No one had bought so much as a bunch all day, and no one had given her even a penny.

Poor little girl! Shivering with cold and hunger she crept along, a perfect picture of misery.

The snowflakes fell on her long blonde hair, which hung down in curls. Lights gleamed in every window, and there came to her the delicious smell of

roast goose, for it was New Year's Eve.

In a corner formed by two houses, she sat down shivering. She drew her little feet under her, but still she grew colder and colder. She did not dare go home until she had sold some matches. If she went home with no money, her father would certainly beat her. And, besides, it was cold enough at home, for they had only the roof above them, and though the largest holes had been blocked with straw and rags, there were many holes left through which the cold wind whistled.

Her little hands were nearly frozen with cold. She couldn't help thinking a single match might do her good if she might only draw it from the bundle, rub it against the wall, and warm her fingers by it. So at last she drew one out and struck it. *Fzzzzit!* It

blazed and burned! It gave out a warm, bright flame like a little candle, as she held one hand and then another over it.

A wonderful little light it was. It really seemed to the little girl as if she sat before a great iron stove with polished brass feet. So blessedly it burned that the little girl stretched out her feet to warm them also. How comfortable she was! But then the flame went out, the stove vanished, and nothing remained but the little burned match in her hand.

She rubbed another match against the wall. It burned brightly, and where the light fell upon the wall it became transparent like a veil, so that she could see through it into the room. A clean white cloth was spread upon the table, on which was a beautiful china dinner service. A roast

goose, stuffed with apples lay upon a platter, sending up wisps of steam and smelling delicious. And then what was still more wonderful, the goose jumped from the dish, with knife and fork still in its breast, and waddled along the floor straight to the little girl.

But then the little match went out, and nothing was left but the thick, damp wall.

She lit another match. And now she was under a most beautiful Christmas tree, larger and far more pretty than the one she had seen through the glass doors at the rich

merchant's. Hundreds of wax candles were burning on the green branches, and bright baubles, such as she had seen in shop windows, twinkled down upon her. The child stretched out her hands to them, then the match went out.

Still the lights of the Christmas tree rose higher and higher. She saw them now as stars in heaven, and one of them fell, forming a long trail of fire.

"Now someone is dying," murmured the little girl softly, for her grandmother, the only person who had loved her, who was now dead, had told her that whenever a star falls a soul flies up to God.

She struck yet another match against the wall, and again it was light. And in the brightness there appeared before her the

little girl's dear old grandmother, bright and radiant, yet kind and sweet, and happy as she had never looked on earth.

"Oh, Grandmother," cried the child, "take me with you. I know you will go away when the match burns out. You, too, will vanish, like the warm stove, the splendid New Year's feast, the beautiful Christmas tree." And in terror that her grandmother should disappear, she rubbed the whole bundle of matches against the wall.

And the matches burned with such a brilliant light that it became brighter than midday. Her grandmother had never looked so beautiful. She took the little girl in her arms, and both flew together, joyously and gloriously, mounting higher and higher, far above the earth. And for them there was neither hunger, nor cold,

nor care – they were with God.

But in the corner, at the dawn of day, sat the little girl, leaning against the wall, stiff and cold, with the matches, one bundle of which was burned.

"She wanted to warm herself, poor little thing," people said. No one imagined what wonderful visions she had had, or how gloriously she had gone with her grandmother to enter upon the joys of a new year.

Little Women's Christmas Breakfast

An extract from *Little Women*
by Louisa May Alcott

*Jo, Meg, Amy and Beth have been told their mother
can't afford any Christmas presents this year, apart from one
dollar each and a book. They've decided to buy presents for their
mother with their money – handkerchiefs, slippers, gloves and
a bottle of cologne. Their father is away at war.*

Jo was the first to wake in the grey dawn of Christmas morning. No stockings hung at the fireplace, and for a moment she felt disappointed. Then she remembered her mother's promise and, slipping her hand under her pillow, drew out a little crimson-covered book. She woke Meg with a 'Merry Christmas' and bade her see what was under her pillow. A green-covered book appeared. Presently Beth and Amy woke to rummage and find their little books also, one dove-coloured, the other blue, and all sat looking at and talking about them, while the east grew rosy with the coming day.

"I'm glad mine is blue," said Amy, and then the rooms were very still while the pages were softly turned, and the winter sunshine crept in to touch the bright heads with a Christmas greeting.

"Where is Mother?" asked Meg, as she and Jo ran down to thank her for their gifts, half an hour later.

"Goodness only knows. Some poor

person came a-beggin', and your ma went straight off to see what was needed. There never was such a woman for givin' away," replied Hannah, who had lived with the family since Meg was born, and was considered by them all more as a friend than a servant.

"She will be back soon, I think, so have everything ready," said Meg, looking over the presents which were collected in a basket and kept under the sofa, ready to be produced at the proper time. "Why, where is Amy's bottle of cologne?" she added, as the little flask did not appear.

"She took it out a minute ago and went off with it to put a ribbon on it, or some such notion," replied Jo, while she danced about the room.

"How nice my handkerchiefs look, don't

they? Hannah washed and ironed them for me, but I marked them all myself," said Beth, looking proudly at the somewhat uneven letters that had cost her such labour.

"Bless the child! She's gone and put 'Mother' on them instead of 'M. March'. How funny!" cried Jo, taking one up.

"Isn't that right? I thought it was better to do it so, because Meg's initials are M.M., and I don't want anyone to use these but Marmee," said Beth, looking troubled.

"It's all right, dear, and a very pretty idea. Quite sensible too, for no one can ever mistake them now. It will please her very much, I know," said Meg, with a frown for Jo and a smile for Beth.

GOODWILL AND GIVING

"There's Mother. Hide the basket, quick!" cried Jo, as a door slammed and steps sounded in the hall.

Amy came in hastily, and saw her sisters all waiting for her.

"Where have you been, and what are you hiding behind you?" asked Meg.

"Don't laugh at me, Jo! I didn't think anyone should know till the time came. I only meant to change the little bottle of cologne for a big one, and I gave all my money to get it."

As she spoke, Amy showed the handsome flask that replaced the cheap one, and looked so earnest that Meg hugged her on the spot, while Beth ran to the window and picked her finest rose to ornament the stately bottle.

Another bang of the street door sent the

basket under the sofa, and the girls to the table, eager for breakfast.

"Merry Christmas, Marmee! Many of them! Thank you for our books," they all cried in chorus.

"Merry Christmas, little daughters. I want to say one word before we sit down. Not far away from here lies a poor woman with a little newborn baby. Six children are huddled into one bed to keep from freezing, for they have no fire. There is nothing to eat over there, and the oldest boy came to tell me they were suffering hunger and cold. My girls, will you give them your breakfast as a Christmas present?"

They were all hungry, having waited nearly an hour, and for a minute no one spoke, but only a minute, for Jo exclaimed, "I'm so glad you came before we began!"

GOODWILL AND GIVING

"May I go and help carry the things to the poor little children?" asked Beth eagerly.

"I shall take the cream and the muffins," added Amy, heroically giving up the article she most liked.

Meg was covering the buckwheats, and piling the bread onto one big plate.

"I thought you'd do it," said Mrs March, smiling as if satisfied. "You shall all come and help me, and when we come back we will have bread and milk for breakfast, and make it up at dinnertime."

They were soon ready, and the little procession set out.

A poor, bare, miserable room it was, with broken windows, no fire, ragged bedclothes, a sick mother, wailing baby, and a group of pale, hungry children cuddled under one old quilt, trying to keep warm.

GOODWILL AND GIVING

How the big eyes stared and the blue lips smiled as the girls went in.

"It is good angels come to us!" said the poor woman, crying for joy.

"Funny angels in hoods and mittens," said Jo, and set them to laughing.

In a few minutes it really did seem as if kind spirits had been at work there. Hannah, who had carried wood, made a fire, and stopped up the broken window panes. Mrs March gave the mother tea and gruel, and comforted her with promises of help, while she dressed the little baby as tenderly as if it had been her own. The girls set the food on the table, sat the children round the fire, and fed them like so many hungry birds, laughing, talking, and trying to understand the funny broken English.

That was a very happy breakfast, though

they didn't get any of it. And when they went away, leaving comfort behind, I think there were not in all the city four merrier people than the hungry little girls who gave away their breakfasts, and contented themselves with only bread and milk on Christmas morning.

"That's loving our neighbour better than ourselves, and I like it," said Meg.

The girls set out their presents while their mother was upstairs collecting clothes for the poor family.

Not a very splendid show, but there was a great deal of love done up in the few little bundles, and the tall vase of red roses, white chrysanthemums and trailing vines, which stood in the middle, gave quite an elegant air to the table.

"She's coming! Strike up, Beth! Open the

door, Amy! Three cheers for Marmee!" cried Jo, prancing about while Meg went to conduct Mother to the seat of honour.

Mrs March was both surprised and touched, and smiled as she examined her presents and read the little notes that accompanied them.

The slippers went on at once, a new handkerchief was slipped into her pocket, well scented with Amy's cologne, the rose was fastened in her bosom, and the nice gloves were pronounced a perfect fit.

Aunt Cyrilla's Christmas Basket

Adapted from a story
by L M Montgomery

When Lucy Rose met Aunt Cyrilla coming downstairs with a big, flat-covered basket hanging over her arm, she gave a little sigh.

"Aunt Cyrilla," she pleaded, "you're surely not going to take that funny old basket to Pembroke – Christmas Day and all."

"I'm not a mite worried about its looks," returned Aunt Cyrilla calmly. "If it hurts your feelings to walk with a countrified old

333

lady with a basket, you can just fall behind."
She nodded and smiled good-humouredly.

"Now, let me see," said Aunt Cyrilla,
"what shall I take? That big fruit cake and
those three mince pies. That plate of jelly
cookies and doughnuts will please the
children, and that ice-cream
candy and the striped candy
sticks. And apples, of
course, two pots of
my greengage
preserves. And
sandwiches and
pound cake for
a snack. The
presents for the
children can go
in on top. There's
a doll for Daisy

and the little boat for Ray. Now, is that all?"

"There's a cold roast chicken in the pantry," said Lucy Rose wickedly.

Aunt Cyrilla smiled broadly. "Since you have reminded me of it, the chicken may as well go in."

Lucy Rose, in spite of her prejudices, helped with the packing and did it very well too. But when Aunt Cyrilla tied the bulging covers down, Lucy Rose stood over the basket and whispered, "Someday I'm going to burn this basket. Then there'll be an end of lugging it everywhere we go."

Uncle Leopold came in just then, shaking his head. "I doubt you folks'll get to Pembroke tomorrow," he said sagely. "It's going to storm."

Next morning Uncle Leopold drove Aunt Cyrilla and Lucy Rose and the basket

to the station, though the air was thick with flying flakes.

When their train came along Aunt Cyrilla looked beamingly around her at her fellow travellers. These were few in number – a delicate little woman with a baby and four other children, a young girl with a pale, pretty face, a sunburnt lad in a khaki uniform, a very handsome old lady in a sealskin coat ahead of him, and a thin young man with spectacles opposite.

"A minister," reflected Aunt Cyrilla, "and that woman in the sealskin is cross at something, and that young chap must be not long out of the hospital."

They expected to reach Pembroke that night, but as the day wore on the storm grew worse. Twice the train had to stop while the train hands dug it out. The third

time it could not go on. It was dusk when the conductor came through the train. "Impossible to go on or back – track blocked for miles – what's that, madam? –

no, no station near. I'm afraid we're here for the night."

"Oh, dear," groaned Lucy Rose.

Aunt Cyrilla looked at her basket. "At any rate, we won't starve," she said.

The sealskin lady looked crosser than ever. The khaki boy said, "Just my luck," and two of the children began to cry. Aunt Cyrilla took some apples and striped candy sticks from her basket. She lifted the oldest into her ample lap and soon had them all around her, laughing and contented.

The rest of the travellers straggled over to the corner and drifted into conversation. The khaki boy said it was hard lines not to get home for Christmas, after all.

"I reached Halifax three days ago and telegraphed the old folks I'd eat my Christmas dinner with them. They'll be

badly disappointed." He looked very disappointed too. Aunt Cyrilla passed him an apple.

"We were all going down to Grandpa's for Christmas," said the little mother's oldest boy. "We've never been there before, and it's just too bad."

The pale, pretty girl came up and took the baby from the tired mother. "What a dear little fellow," she said softly.

"Are you going home for Christmas too?" asked Aunt Cyrilla.

The girl shook her head. "I'm just a shop girl out of work at present, and I'm going to Pembroke to look for some."

Aunt Cyrilla went to her basket and took out her box of cream candy. "I guess we might as well enjoy ourselves. Let's have a good time."

GOODWILL AND GIVING

The little group grew cheerful as they nibbled, and even the sealskin lady brightened up.

By and by the children fell asleep. Aunt Cyrilla and the pale girl helped the mother make up beds for them.

"We must get up some Santa Claus stuff for these youngsters," said the khaki boy. "Let's hang their stockings on the wall and fill them up as best we can. I've nothing about me but some cash and a knife. I'll give each of them a quarter and the boy can have the knife."

"I've nothing but money either," said the sealskin lady.

Aunt Cyrilla glanced at the little mother. She had fallen asleep.

"I've got a basket over there," said Aunt Cyrilla firmly, "and I've some presents in it.

I'm going to give them to these. As for the money, I think the mother is the one for it to go to. Let's make up a little purse among us for a Christmas present."

The khaki boy passed his cap and everybody contributed. The sealskin lady put in a note for twenty dollars.

Meanwhile, Lucy Rose had brought the basket. She smiled at Aunt Cyrilla as she lugged it down the aisle, and Aunt Cyrilla smiled back. Lucy Rose had never touched that basket of her own accord before.

Ray's boat went to Jacky, and Daisy's doll to his oldest sister. Then the stockings were filled up with doughnuts and jelly cookies, and the money was put in an envelope and pinned to the mother's jacket.

When morning came the storm was still raging. The children wakened and went

wild with delight over their stockings. The little mother found her envelope and tried to utter her thanks. Then the conductor came in and told them they'd be spending Christmas on the train.

Aunt Cyrilla rose to the occasion.

"I've got some emergency rations here," she announced. "There's plenty for all and we'll have our Christmas dinner, although a cold one. Breakfast first thing. There's a sandwich apiece left, and we

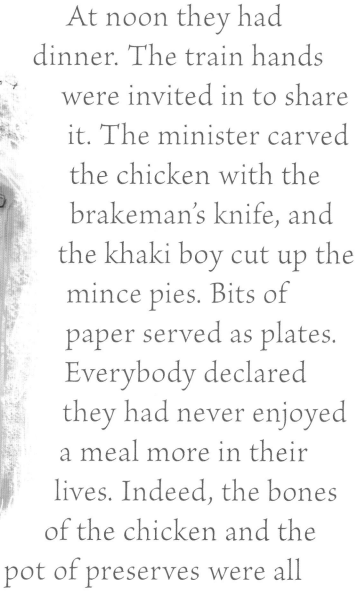

must fill up on what is left of the cookies and doughnuts."

At noon they had dinner. The train hands were invited in to share it. The minister carved the chicken with the brakeman's knife, and the khaki boy cut up the mince pies. Bits of paper served as plates. Everybody declared they had never enjoyed a meal more in their lives. Indeed, the bones of the chicken and the pot of preserves were all that was left. And when two hours later the conductor came in and said they'd

soon be starting, they all wondered if it could really be less than twenty-four hours since they met.

At the next station they all parted. The little mother and the children had to take the next train back home. The minister stayed there, and the khaki boy and the sealskin lady changed trains. The sealskin lady shook Aunt Cyrilla's hand. She no longer looked cross.

"This has been the pleasantest Christmas I have ever spent," she said heartily. "I shall never forget that wonderful basket of yours. The little shop girl is going home with me, and I've promised her a place in my husband's store."

When Aunt Cyrilla and Lucy Rose reached Pembroke there was nobody there to meet them because everyone had given

up expecting them, so Aunt Cyrilla elected to walk.

"I'll carry the basket," said Lucy Rose. "It's a blessed old basket and I love it. Please forget all the silly things I ever said about it, Aunt Cyrilla."

The Christmas Cuckoo

Adapted from a story
by Frances Browne

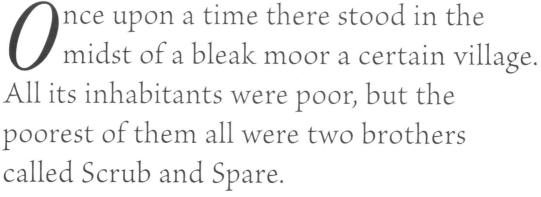

*O*nce upon a time there stood in the midst of a bleak moor a certain village. All its inhabitants were poor, but the poorest of them all were two brothers called Scrub and Spare.

When Christmas came they had nothing to feast on but a barley loaf and a piece of bacon. Worse than that, the snow was very deep and they could get no firewood.

Their hut stood at the end of the village.

Beyond it spread the bleak moor, now all white and silent. But that moor had once been a forest – great roots of old trees were still to be found in it. One of these, a rough, gnarled log, lay by their door, and Spare said to his brother, "Shall we sit here cold on Christmas while the great root lies yonder? Let us chop it up for firewood. The work will make us warm."

In hopes of having a fine yule log, both brothers strained and strove with all their might until, between pulling and pushing, the great old root was safe on the hearth, and beginning to crackle and blaze with the red embers.

In high glee the cobblers sat down to their bread and bacon. The door was shut, but the hut looked cheerful as the blaze flared up.

Then suddenly from within the blazing root they heard, "Cuckoo! Cuckoo!"

"What is that?" said Scrub, terribly frightened.

And out of the deep hole at the side of the root, which the fire had not yet reached, flew a large, grey cuckoo, which said, "Good gentlemen, what season is this?"

"It's Christmas," said Spare.

"Then a Merry Christmas to you!" said the cuckoo. "I went to sleep in the hollow of that old root one evening last summer, and never woke till the heat of your fire made me think it was summer again. Let me stay in your hut till the spring comes round – and when I go on my travels next summer I

will bring you some present."

"Stay and welcome," said Spare. "I'll make you a good warm hole in the thatch. But you must be hungry after that long sleep – here is a slice of barley bread."

The cuckoo ate up the slice and flew into a snug hole, which Spare scooped for it in the thatch of the hut.

So the snow melted, the heavy rains came, the cold grew less, and one sunny morning the brothers were awakened by the cuckoo shouting its own cry to let them know the spring had come.

"Now I'm going on my travels," said the bird, "over the world to tell men of the spring. Give me another slice of barley bread, and tell me what present I shall bring you at the twelvemonth's end."

Scrub's mind was occupied with what

present to ask for.

"There are two trees hard by the well that lies at the world's end," said the cuckoo. "One of them is called the golden tree, for its leaves are all of beaten gold. As for the other, it is always green like a laurel. Its leaves never fall, but they that get one keep a cheerful heart in spite of all misfortunes."

"Good cuckoo, bring me a leaf off that tree!" cried Spare.

"Now, brother, don't be a fool!" said Scrub. "Think of the leaves of beaten gold! Dear cuckoo, bring me one of them!"

Before another word could be spoken the cuckoo had flown out of the open door.

So the seasons came and passed – spring, summer, harvest, and winter followed each other. At daybreak on the First of April the brothers heard a beak knocking at their

door, and a voice crying, "Cuckoo! Cuckoo! Let me in with my presents!"

Spare ran to open the door, and in came the cuckoo, carrying on one side of its beak a golden leaf, and in the other, one like that of the common laurel, only a fresher green.

"Here," it said, giving the gold to Scrub and the green to Spare.

So much gold had never been in the cobbler's hands before. "See the wisdom of my choice," he said, holding up the large leaf of gold.

"Good master cobbler," cried the cuckoo. "If your brother is disappointed this time, I go on the same journey every year, and I will bring each of you whichever leaf you most desire."

"Bring me a golden one," cried Scrub.

And Spare said, "Be sure to bring me one

from the merry tree."

And away flew the cuckoo.

"This is the feast of All Fools, and it ought to be your birthday," said Scrub. "Did ever man fling away such an opportunity of getting rich?"

But Spare laughed at him till Scrub, at length getting angry, vowed his brother was not fit to live with a respectable man, and he left the hut and went to tell the villagers.

They were charmed with Scrub's good sense, particularly when he showed them the golden leaf, and told that the cuckoo would bring him one every spring.

Fairfeather, a beautiful village maiden, smiled upon him, and in the course of that summer they were married, with a grand wedding feast, at which the whole village danced except Spare, who was not invited,

because his brother thought him a disgrace to the family.

Spare lived on in the old hut, and worked in the cabbage garden. Every day his coat grew more ragged, but people often remarked that he never looked sad or sour. And the wonder was that, from the time anyone began to keep his company, he or she grew kinder, happier, and content.

Every first of April the cuckoo came tapping at their doors with the golden leaf for Scrub, and the green leaf for Spare. Scrub spent the golden leaves, and remained always discontented, and Spare kept the merry ones.

GOODWILL AND GIVING

I do not know how many years passed in this manner, when a certain great lord, who owned that village, came to the neighbourhood. His castle stood on the moor, and there he lived in a very bad temper. The servants said nothing would please him.

But one day, His Lordship chanced to meet Spare gathering watercresses at a meadow stream, and fell into talk with the cobbler. How it was nobody could tell, but from that hour the great lord forgot all his woes, and went about hunting, fishing, and making merry in his hall, where all the poor were welcome.

This strange story spread through the North Country, and great company came to talk with Spare, and, whatever their troubles had been, all went home merry.

The rich gave him presents, the poor gave him thanks. Spare had bacon with his cabbage, and the villagers began to think there was some sense in him.

By this time his fame had reached the capital city, and even the court. So a royal messenger was sent to Spare, with a diamond ring, and a command that he should go to court immediately.

His coming caused great surprise there. Everybody wondered what the king could see in such a common-looking man. But scarcely had His Majesty talked with Spare half an hour, when orders were given that a feast should be spread in the banquet hall.

The great lords and ladies then all talked with Spare, and the more they talked the lighter grew their hearts, so that such changes had never been seen at court.

GOODWILL AND GIVING

As for Spare, he had a chamber assigned to him in the palace, and a seat at the king's table. He continued to live at the king's court, happy and honoured, and making all others merry and content.

Mr Dog Plays Santa Claus

An extract from *How Mr Rabbit Lost his Tail*
by Albert Bigelow Paine

*Mr Dog lives close to the Hollow Tree,
the home of his woodland animal friends.*

Once upon a time the Robin and Turtle and Squirrel and Jack Rabbit had all gone home for the winter, and nobody was left in the Hollow Tree except the 'Coon and 'Possum and the Old Black Crow. Of course the others used to come back and visit them pretty often, and Mr Dog, too.

GOODWILL AND GIVING

Mr Dog told them a lot of things they had never heard of before, things that he'd learned at Mr Man's house, and maybe that's one reason why they got to liking him so well.

He told them about Santa Claus, for one thing, and how the old fellow came down the chimney on Christmas Eve to bring presents to Mr Man and his children, who always hung up their stockings for them. And Mr Dog said that once he had hung up his stocking, too, and got a nice bone in it.

Well, the Hollow Tree people had never heard of Santa Claus. They knew about Christmas, of course, because everybody, even the cows and sheep, know about that, but they had never heard of Santa Claus. They thought if they just hung up their stockings he'd come there, too, and that's

what they made up their minds to do.

They talked about it a great deal together, and Mr 'Possum looked over all his stockings to pick out the biggest one he had, and Mr Crow made himself a new pair on purpose.

When Mr Dog heard about it he wanted to laugh right out. You see, he knew Santa Claus never went anywhere except to Mr Man's house, and he thought it would be a great joke on the Hollow Tree people when they hung up their stockings and didn't get anything.

But by and by Mr Dog thought it would

359

be too bad for them to be disappointed that way. You see, Mr Dog liked them all, and when he had thought about that a minute, he made up his mind to play Santa Claus!

Well, he had to work pretty hard to get things ready. He found some long wool out in Mr Man's barn for his white beard, and he put some that wasn't so long on the edges of his overcoat and boot tops, and around an old hat. Then he borrowed a big sack he found out there, too, and fixed it up to swing over his back, just as he had seen Santa Claus do in the pictures.

He had a lot of nice things to take along. Three tender young chickens he'd borrowed from Mr Man, for one thing, and then he bought some new neckties for the Hollow Tree folks, and a big, striped candy cane for each one, because candy canes always

looked good sticking out of a stocking. He had even more things than that, but I can't remember just now what they were, and when he started out, all dressed up like Santa Claus, his bag was pretty heavy.

It got heavier and heavier all the way, and Mr Dog was glad enough to get there and find the latch string out. He set his bag down to rest a minute before climbing the stairs, and then he opened the door softly and listened. He didn't hear a thing except Mr Crow and Mr 'Coon and Mr 'Possum breathing pretty low, and he knew they might wake up any minute, and

he wouldn't have been caught there in the midst of things for a good deal.

So he slipped up just as easy as anything, and when he got to the big parlour room there were the stockings, all hung up in a row, and a card with a name on it over each one, telling who it belonged to.

So then he opened his bag, took down the stockings and filled them. He put in mixed candy and nuts and little things first, and then the candy canes, so they would show at the top. I tell you, they looked fine! It almost made Mr Dog wish he had a stocking of his own there to fill, and he forgot all about them waking up, and sat down in a chair to look at the stockings.

It was a nice rocking chair, and over in a dark corner where they wouldn't see him, even if one of them did wake up and stick

his head out of his room, so Mr Dog felt pretty safe now, anyway. He rocked softly, and looked at the nice stockings, and thought how pleased they'd be in the morning, and how tired he was. You've heard about people being as tired as a dog, and that's just how Mr Dog felt. He was so tired he didn't feel a bit like starting home, and by and by Mr Dog went sound asleep right there in his chair, with all his Santa Claus clothes on.

And there he sat, with his empty bag in his hand and the nice full stockings in front of him, all night long. Even when it became morning and began to get light, Mr Dog just slept right on, he was that tired.

Then the door of Mr 'Possum's room opened and he poked out his head. Then the door of Mr 'Coon's room opened and he

poked out his head. Then the door of
Mr Crow's room opened and he poked out
his head. They all looked towards the
stockings, and they didn't see Mr Dog, or
even each other. They saw their stockings,
though, and Mr 'Coon said all at once, "Oh,
there's something in my stocking!"

And then Mr Crow said, "Oh, there's
something in my stocking, too!"

And Mr 'Possum said, "Oh, there's
something in all our stockings!"

And with that they gave a great hurrah
all together, and rushed out and grabbed
their stockings. They turned around just in
time to see Mr Dog jump straight up out of
his chair, for he did not know where he was
the least bit in the world.

"Oh, there's Santa Claus himself!" they
all shouted together, and made a rush for

their rooms, for they were scared almost to death. Then it all dawned on Mr Dog in a second, and he started to laugh. And when they heard Mr Dog laugh they knew him right away, and they all came up and looked at him, and he had to tell just what he'd done and everything.

So they emptied out their stockings on the floor and ate some of the presents and looked at the others, until they almost forgot about breakfast, just as children do on Christmas morning.

Scrooge Celebrates Christmas

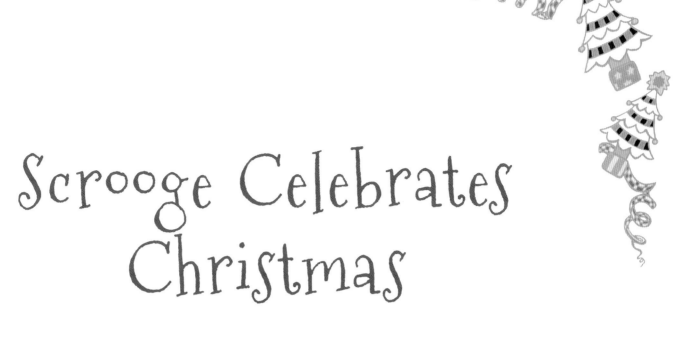

An extract from *A Christmas Carol*
by Charles Dickens

*Ebenezer Scrooge has been shown by three ghosts what
a mean man he has been, especially to his clerk, Bob Cratchit,
and his nephew Fred. Scrooge has always hated Christmas, but
the ghosts have shown him what a wonderful season it is.
Now he has woken up, determined to do better.*

"I don't know what day of the month it is!" said Scrooge. "I don't know how long I've been among the Spirits. I don't know anything. I'm quite a baby. Never mind. I don't care. I'd rather be a baby. Hallo!

Whoop! Hallo here!"

He was checked by the churches ringing out the lustiest peals he had ever heard. *Clash, clang, hammer! Ding, dong! Dong, ding! Hammer, clang, clash!* Oh, glorious, glorious!

Running to the window, he opened it and put out his head. No fog, no mist – clear, bright, jovial, stirring. Cold – cold, piping for the blood to dance to. Golden sunlight, heavenly sky, sweet fresh air, merry bells. Oh, glorious! Glorious!

"What's today?" cried Scrooge, calling downwards to a boy in Sunday clothes.

"Today?" replied the boy. "Why, it's Christmas Day."

"It's Christmas Day!" said Scrooge. "I haven't missed it. Hallo, my fine fellow!"

"Hallo!" returned the boy.

"Do you know the Poulterer's, in the next

street but one, at the corner?" Scrooge
asked the boy.

"I should hope I did,"
replied the lad.

"An intelligent boy!" said
Scrooge. "A remarkable boy!
Do you know whether they've
sold the turkey that was
hanging up there? Not the
little prize one – the big one?"

"What, the one as big as me?"
returned the boy.

"What a delightful boy!" said
Scrooge. "It's a pleasure to talk to
him. Yes, my boy!"

"It's hanging there now," replied the boy.

"Is it?" said Scrooge. "Go and buy it, and
tell 'em to bring it here. Come back with
the man, and I'll give you a shilling. Come

back with him in less than five minutes and I'll give you half a crown!"

The boy was off like a shot. "I'll send it to Bob Cratchit's!" whispered Scrooge, rubbing his hands, and splitting with a laugh. "He shan't know who sends it."

The boy returned, staggering under the weight of the enormous turkey!

"Why, it's impossible to carry that to Camden Town," said Scrooge. "You must have a cab."

The chuckle with which he said this, and the chuckle with which he paid for the turkey, and the chuckle with which he paid for the cab, and the chuckle with which he paid the boy, were only exceeded by the chuckle with which he sat down breathless in his chair again, and chuckled till he cried.

He dressed himself all in his best, and at

last got out into the streets. The people were by this time pouring forth and Scrooge regarded every one with a delighted smile. He looked so pleasant, that three or four good-humoured fellows said, "Good morning, sir! A Merry Christmas to you!"

He went to church, and walked about the streets, and watched the people hurrying to and fro, and patted children on the head, and conversed

with beggars. He had never dreamed that any walk – that anything – could give him such happiness. In the afternoon he turned his steps towards his nephew's house.

He passed the door a dozen times, before he had the courage to go up and knock. But then he made a dash and did it.

"Is your master at home, my dear?" said Scrooge to the girl. Nice girl!

"Yes, sir."

"Where is he, my love?" said Scrooge.

"He's in the dining room, sir, along with mistress," the girl replied.

"Thank'ee. He knows me," said Scrooge. "I'll go in, my dear."

He turned the handle of the dining room door gently, and sidled his face in, round the door.

"Fred!" said Scrooge.

"Why bless my soul!" cried Fred, "who is that?"

"It's I. Your uncle Scrooge. I have come to dinner. Will you let me in, Fred?"

Let him in! It is a mercy he didn't shake his arm off. He was made to feel at home in five minutes. Wonderful party, wonderful games, wonderful happiness!

But he was early at the office next morning. Oh, he was early there. If he could only be there first, and catch Bob Cratchit coming late! That was the thing he had set his heart upon.

And he did it, yes, he did! The clock struck nine. No Bob. A quarter past. No Bob. He was full eighteen minutes and a half behind his time. Scrooge sat with his door wide open, that he might see him come in.

Bob's hat was off, before he opened the door, his comforter too. He was on his stool in a jiffy, driving away with his pen, as if he were trying to overtake nine o'clock.

"Hallo!" growled Scrooge. "What do you mean by coming here at this time of day?"

"I am very sorry, sir," said Bob. "I am behind my time."

"You are?" repeated Scrooge. "Yes. I think you are. Step this way, sir, if you please."

"It's only once a year, sir," pleaded Bob. "It shall not be repeated. I was making rather merry yesterday, sir."

"Now, I'll tell you what, my friend," said Scrooge. "I am not going to stand this sort of thing any longer. And therefore," he continued, leaping from his stool, "and therefore I am about to raise your salary!"

Bob trembled.

"A Merry Christmas, Bob!" said Scrooge, with an earnestness that could not be mistaken, as he clapped him on the back. "A merrier Christmas, Bob, my good fellow, than I have given you, for many a year! I'll raise your salary, and endeavour to assist your struggling family, and we will discuss your affairs this very afternoon."

Scrooge was better than his word. He did it all, and infinitely more. He became as good a friend, as good a master, and as good a man, as the good old city knew, or any other good old city in the good old world.

GOODWILL AND GIVING

Some people laughed to see the alteration in him, but he let them laugh, for he was wise enough to know that nothing ever happened on this globe, for good, at which some people did not have their fill of laughter in the outset.

His own heart laughed and that was quite enough for him and it was always said of him, that he knew how to keep Christmas well, if any man alive possessed the knowledge. May that be truly said of us, and all of us!

The Twelve Days of Christmas

Traditional

On the first day of Christmas
my true love sent to me:
A partridge in a pear tree

On the second day of Christmas
my true love sent to me:
Two turtle doves
and a partridge in a pear tree

GOODWILL AND GIVING

On the third day of Christmas
my true love sent to me:
Three French hens
Two turtle doves
and a partridge in a pear tree

On the fourth day of Christmas
my true love sent to me:
Four calling birds
Three French hens
Two turtle doves
and a partridge in a pear tree

On the fifth day of Christmas
my true love sent to me:
Five golden rings
Four calling birds
Three French hens
Two turtle doves
and a partridge in a pear tree

The Twelve Days of Christmas

On the sixth day of Christmas
my true love sent to me:
Six geese a-laying
Five golden rings
Four calling birds
Three French hens
Two turtle doves
and a partridge in a pear tree

On the seventh day of Christmas
my true love sent to me:
Seven swans a-swimming
Six geese a-laying
Five golden rings
Four calling birds
Three French hens
Two turtle doves
and a partridge in a pear tree

379

GOODWILL AND GIVING

On the eighth day of Christmas
my true love sent to me:
Eight maids a-milking
Seven swans a-swimming
Six geese a-laying
Five golden rings
Four calling birds
Three French hens
Two turtle doves
and a partridge in a pear tree

On the ninth day of Christmas
my true love sent to me:
Nine ladies dancing
Eight maids a-milking
Seven swans a-swimming
Six geese a-laying
Five golden rings
Four calling birds
Three French hens
Two turtle doves
and a partridge in a pear tree

The Twelve Days of Christmas

On the tenth day of Christmas
my true love sent to me:
Ten lords a-leaping
Nine ladies dancing
Eight maids a-milking
Seven swans a-swimming
Six geese a-laying
Five golden rings
Four calling birds
Three French hens
Two turtle doves
and a partridge in a pear tree

GOODWILL AND GIVING

On the eleventh day of Christmas
my true love sent to me:
Eleven pipers piping
Ten lords a-leaping
Nine ladies dancing
Eight maids a-milking
Seven swans a-swimming
Six geese a-laying
Five golden rings
Four calling birds
Three French hens
Two turtle doves
and a partridge in a pear tree

The Twelve Days of Christmas

On the twelfth day of Christmas
my true love sent to me:
Twelve drummers drumming
Eleven pipers piping
Ten lords a-leaping
Nine ladies dancing
Eight maids a-milking
Seven swans a-swimming
Six geese a-laying
Five golden rings
Four calling birds
Three French hens
Two turtle doves
and a partridge in a pear tree

The End